Running Into You

A Ridgefield Romance

JLynn Autumn

Contents

Cover Design: Lauren Hanson
Chapter Headers & Graphic Designs: Lauren Hanson
Book Formatting: J.L. Dunn
Book Editing: Kristy Perkins

Trigger Warnings

Breath play, restraints, gagging, edging, and orgasm denial. The combat-injured ex-military hero experiences symptoms consistent with PTSD but is undiagnosed.

 *Dedication*

Dear Mom (or any parent-like person in my life),
Let's not make family events awkward. Please don't read
this.

Author's Note

Running Into You was originally published as *Chef's Kiss* in the *Love Under Fire* anthology in 2024. This is the expanded version of that short story. It contains additional scenes and chapters. It also introduces new characters that are part of the *Ridgefield* series. While it is the second book published in the *Ridgefield* series, it is the first in timeline order.

Please note, I primarily write books in past tense. This is a rare occasion where I chose present tense. I know there are varying opinions on this, but for this story, to accurately portray the MMC's struggle with undiagnosed PTSD, it worked better in present tense. For my past tense only readers, please give this story a chance.

Chapter 1

What would my shrink say if she knew I found comfort in the camo green bouncy ball's cadence as it hits my ceiling, lands in my hand, and then launches into the air again? Probably something about how I need to find an outlet. That my insomnia is because I'm not talking about anything. She'd suggest another group meeting. It isn't that I don't see the value in those programs, but I feel like a fraud sitting in a room with other soldiers talking about my problems when I had it so much better than anyone else in those rooms. Six herniated disks, hip surgery, and knee reconstruction weren't a lost limb or life in a wheelchair. I didn't have chronic headaches or nightmares. From the outside, my life looked great. A post-discharge career is possible. My hobbies are still accessible—running, hiking, and mountain biking are all regular things in my life. But it doesn't feel like my life because the injury stole the future I'd mapped out for myself when I was fifteen.

Bounce.

995.

Bounce.

996.

Bounce.

997.

The last time I sat in a group therapy room, I never said a word because I felt like utter shit for not being thankful for everything I had, while everyone else had lost so much more. I shake the memories of the day my life changed from my mind and focus on the green sphere flying in the air and tapping the ceiling.

Bounce.

998.

Bounce.

999.

Bounce.

1,000.

This time, when the ball lands in my hand, I set it on my nightstand. If my upstairs neighbors were home, they would hate me. I'm on night ten of little to no sleep. I've spent the evenings pacing across the basement studio and bouncing ping-pong and bouncy balls off the walls and ceiling. Whatever routine I've fallen into the last six months isn't my life. At least it's not the life I want.

Six months ago, after almost two years of physical therapy, I exhausted my appeals. The decision was final. I would never pass the physical requirements for my job and could no longer deploy to combat zones. The goal of military retirement was gone. All the work I put into my training and education seemed pointless. I've spent the last six months living in my younger brother's basement—a temporary fix to my lack of housing and an opportunity to figure out what I want to do now.

What I want to do is continue working in counterintelligence and put my language skills to use. I grew up in a bilingual household, speaking English and Spanish. I studied Russian in high school and college, then studied Arabic at the Defense Language Institute Foreign Language Center in Monterey while in the Marines. My language skills were valuable in the Marines but didn't do much for me in the civilian world.

Unfortunately, my injury means I can't pass the physical for any law enforcement agency, not even for a desk job. My sister-in-law is a high school counselor and convinced me to get my substitute credential because they needed subs and I needed to get out of the house. I know she hopes I'll agree to take the foreign language teacher position at the school, but subbing taught me one thing—teenagers are horrible. Well, maybe it's not the teens. It's the lack of basic respect. I blame that on their parents.

My eyes shift to my cell phone. Maybe Devin is right. I need to go home. Not my hometown, living in my brother's basement, but the state that became my home while attending Ridgefield University and while stationed at Pendleton. I pick up my phone and open the message. For anyone else, midnight on a weekday is too late to text, but Devin owns a restaurant with a bar and they close at two.

> If you're serious about the offer, I'll take the job and the spare room. Fair warning, I'm a shit roommate with serious insomnia. I pace the halls until 2 or 3 each night.

I know it's been over a decade since we worked together, but have you forgotten? A kitchen might close at midnight, but that doesn't mean you're out of there. Plus, I plan to get you behind the bar some nights. Figure out when you can get here and let me know.

> I'll hit the road on Monday. Give my family one more Sunday night dinner, and I'll be in Ridgefield on Wednesday. I can start working on Thursday.

Isn't that a little soon? Won't your family want more time with you?

They all know I'm going stir-crazy. My parents already asked about my plans. I told them I was seriously considering your offer. My brother and his wife both made me promise not to bail while they were gone. Everyone knows I'm ready for a change.

Plan on starting the next week. Give yourself a couple days to get acquainted with the area again.

Sounds good. Any house or work rules I need to know about?

I'll go over restaurant shit when I train you. My house rules are simple, if you bring a guest back to the house, make sure they leave before you do. Clean up your stuff. And don't date my sister.

Marines drilled the cleaning and organizing thing into me. No problem. I hate hookups. On the rare occasion they happen, I get a hotel room. I'm not looking to date. Those rules aren't an issue. See you middle of next week. I'll keep you posted on my drive.

Chapter 2

I get into Ridgefield about an hour earlier than I expected, so I decide to drive through the downtown area and get a feel for how much has changed since I was here for Devin's restaurant opening. Next month is Forkn Spoon's tenth anniversary.

Devin told me he had a meeting at the bank and would meet me for lunch at noon. I park my Expedition in the public lot across from the restaurant and send a quick message to Devin.

I'm in town earlier than expected. Just parked. I'm gonna walk through downtown and see what's changed. Call me when you're done and let me know where to meet you. I know you said you wanted to eat somewhere other than the restaurant.

Should be done in about 20 minutes. Go get in line at Wok the Boat. We can grab all-you-can-eat sushi and catch up. Their ramen lunch special is fantastic if you're not in the mood for sushi.

Sounds great. See you there.

I walk the two blocks to the restaurant and take in all the changes to Ridgefield. The buildings all look the same from the outside. A mix of senior citizens, families, and college students fills the outdoor areas. About half the businesses are the same. Others are the same type of business with a new name. My favorite pizza shop is no longer Slices. Instead, it's Slice of Life. It's still a walk-up window with the daily offerings written on a chalkboard. I stop to look over the menu and realize they serve more than pizza now. Pizza, cake, and pie by the slice is a fantastic idea. I've never been one to think dessert has to happen after a meal, so I buy a slice of strawberry lemonade cake to enjoy on my walk and while I wait in line for the sushi buffet. Wok the Boat is notorious for a line forming at least half an hour before they open, so

I'm not surprised to have over twenty people ahead of me.

I lean against the brick wall and people-watch while I enjoy the tart lemon cake with strawberry whipped cream frosting and layers of strawberry puree. The best entertainment is across the street. My favorite dive bar is now Pour Me Another. The sign out front has a list of new beers and wines, so I assume it's now a beer and wine tasting room. I had the good sense to check the University's calendar and know the next quarter starts Monday. Bars and tasting rooms packed with drunk college students in the middle of the afternoon aren't a regular occurrence, but it's common after finals and on breaks between quarters. Work hard so you can party harder was definitely my motto at one time. Apparently, it's still a popular way of thinking.

A group of four girls, all in their early- to mid-twenties, exit Pour Me Another. They stand out from the others because they're dressed in what girls my age called 'going out tops' when we were in college. Skin-tight jeans for three of them and tight black pants for the fourth, paired with low-cut tops and heels with perfect hair and makeup. They look like they are ready for a night at the club, not a mid-week afternoon beer. But something about the brunette captivates my attention. She has definitely had a few drinks, not so much that she is stumbling drunk, but enough that she is feeling the effects of the alcohol. She stops next to the light pole, places her hand on it, and goes through a series of ballet poses before spinning in a circle. She is slightly off balance and catches herself before stumbling over.

Her laugh is contagious. She not only sends her trio of friends into giggles, but I find myself chuckling too.

To the tune of *Take Me to Church*, the captivating brunette sings, "Take me to cake," and I swear my heart leaps. Why? I'm not sure. And it does it again when she darts across the street and stops in front of me.

She peers into my takeout container. "Is that strawberry lemonade cake?"

"It sure is." I know I'm staring, but I can't help myself. There's something about her that makes me want to get to know her. It's not just her beauty. It's her contagious smile and laughter. And the way she lightens my mood just by being in my presence. I am not the guy who smiles a goofy grin or chuckles when he people-watches, but I've done those things today. It makes me wonder if she has this effect on everyone, or just me. I can't help but hope it's just me. She's far too young for me though, so I quickly push that thought from my mind.

"It's my favorite. I'm heading that way right now."

I tap my fork against the half slice remaining in the pink cardboard box. "Sorry to be the bearer of bad news, but this was the last slice."

"Noooo," she whines with an adorable foot stomp. "How? It's not even noon."

"The guy ahead of me bought two whole cakes and the half from this one. I lucked out. He left a single slice."

She tosses her head back and lets out a sigh, "That is so incredibly unfair. If you want a full cake, you're supposed to order in advance. I think I might cry. I have to work all day on Saturday and won't have time to get there. Strawberry lemonade is only available on

Wednesdays and Saturdays. I have to wait an entire week."

Before I realize what I'm doing, I hold out the cotton candy pink box. "I'll split it with you. It was an impulse purchase and I'm meeting a friend for lunch."

She steps toward me and places her hand on my forearm. "And here I thought you were hired to hold up the brick wall and make it look sexy. Tattoo-covered human statues could sure bring a new look to this town."

"I'm certain the city council wouldn't go for that idea. When I lived here, there was a protest when a second tattoo shop wanted to open."

Her brown eyes sparkle when she bursts into laughter. "I remember that. I think I was seven. Blast from the past with Ridgefield town history right there. There are three shops now. The original is still the best."

I remove her hand from my forearm, roll up my sleeve, and point to the eagle on my arm. "Dan did this one."

"Dan, Dan, the tattoo man is the best! He's the only one allowed to tattoo me. But he's preparing to retire and his niece will run the shop. She's pretty kick-ass, so I might let her do my next piece." She snags the box from my hand. "I will take you up on your offer for splitting this cake. Are you back in town for a while? Maybe we can meet for a drink? My treat as a thank you for this."

"I'm back in town as of today. The drink isn't necessary. Now I have room for ramen and sushi."

She takes backward steps toward the trio of friends watching us from the corner. "Well, in that case, I guess I'll see you around. Unless you want my name and number."

I spend too much time watching her take a bite of the cake before responding. I want her name and number, but I'm not accepting. Between the age difference and me not knowing how long I'll stick around town, it's too complicated. "I'm a fan of serendipity. Chance meetings. Unexpected reunions. All that jazz."

She licks the frosting from the fork. "So you're not even going to tell me your name?"

"Nope. Not today."

"How about a hint?"

If I was ten years younger, even five years, I wouldn't be talking myself out of giving her my name, finding out hers, and making plans with her. Hell, I'd ditch Devin and tell him I'd see him at the house or restaurant later. The correct thing to do is let her walk away, but I can't make myself do it. I give in to her request. "I'm named after my mom's favorite mythical creature."

As she reaches her friends, she calls out, "Bye Mr. Sexy Pegasus or unicorn or whatever you are. I'm gonna figure it out. And if you change your mind and want to find me, here's your hint. I'm a fan of all things risky and risqué." With that, she turns and joins her friends. If I was a better man, I wouldn't stare at her ass until she turns the corner, but I totally do. And I let my eyes linger on the corner, secretly hoping she'll come back in sight. But she doesn't.

Risky and risqué? What could that mean?

I don't have much time to think about it because Devin approaches me from the other direction. My best friend greets me with a quick fist bump, followed immediately by a hug. It doesn't surprise me when he uses my last name. Between sports and JROTC in high school, ROTC in college, and my days in service, hardly anyone outside of my family uses my first name. "Hey, Jameson. Great to see you, man. I know it's been a bit since you've been here, but most people step forward as the line moves."

"Sorry, I was fully distracted in people-watching," I reply as I step forward the five or six spots that had moved while I was too focused on the brunette bombshell that I'm definitely not going to search for any time soon.

After lunch, Devin and I head toward the public parking lot. "Thanks again for the job and a place to crash."

"No problem. The spare room is yours as long as you want it—a month, a year, or two years. Rent is still ridiculous around here because students need housing."

"What happened to the new dorms they were supposed to build after I graduated?"

"They built them, then expanded admissions. You're only guaranteed housing in your first and second year. After that, off-campus or lotto for an on-campus apartment is your only choice. A lot of my part-time staff are college students. They're putting at least two, if not three, people in bedrooms to afford rent. I think one mentioned six people sharing a two-bedroom."

That sounded awful, but then again, I'd spent years sharing worse living situations while deployed, so anything would be better than that. The barracks were a lot like college dorms and eventually, I had a high enough rank to have my own room.

During lunch, after I told him the details about my physical therapy and rehab, Devin caught me up on his life. He was currently married to his restaurant and too busy for a relationship. He gave me some basic details about his sister Sadie and told me I'd meet her soon. But he hadn't mentioned his folks at all. Other than knowing his dad retired from the university a few years ago, I didn't know anything about him. "Where's your pops at now?"

"Lives at the cabin in Tahoe year-round."

"And your mom?"

His shoulders practically touch his ears as he shoves his hands into his pockets. I know from that his relationship with his mom hasn't changed. "Her new husband owns a house in Merced. She hauled ass in that direction the day she dropped the unexpected divorce announcement. Sadie was still living at home. She had just turned sixteen. Mom told her she could move to Merced. Sadie told her to fuck off. She stayed in town, finished high school early, and went to cosmetology school as soon as she could. She does hair and makeup for a local theater group and runs her own special event hair and makeup company."

It's weird to think about Sadie as an adult. The last time I saw her was at the restaurant opening. She had just turned thirteen and was incredibly shy. She kept her freckle-covered nose hidden in a book at the table closest to the kitchen. I don't think she said a word to anyone that night. Devin and I are the type of friends who keep each other posted on our lives, but don't share much about our families. I'm not on social media other than a private Instagram account that I only have because my brother set it up for me so I could follow our family members and see pictures of everyone. I think I've posted ten photos in the last three years. "Hmm. Not sure I would have ever guessed she'd end up in theater, hair, and makeup."

"She's not the freckle-faced, shy little girl anymore. She's an older brother's nightmare. Goddamn knockout, social butterfly, and wild. The girl lives for adventure. She hated every minute of high school because she never found her place to belong. She found her people and her passion in cosmetology school. Within six months, we saw her break out of her shell. By the time she finished the coursework, you couldn't recognize her—in the best possible way. She did her apprenticeship with one of the owners of the theater she works for now. The theater was a pipe dream, but when it happened, Sadie was instantly brought into it. Dad offered her the house when he decided to move to Tahoe, but she wanted to do it on her own. She lives in a house with friends from the theater. Her roommate Olivia got the house in her divorce, and some friends moved in to help her keep it. My sister is big on no handouts from anyone. That's what she told me when I offered the second bedroom in my place."

I respect that. That type of mindset is how I ended up in JROTC in high school with my eye on the prize for my career goal. I did everything possible to follow the path the recruiters helped me map because I was determined to do it on my own. Moreso, I knew there was only a little money for college and wanted my siblings to have it. I figured out a way to do it without being a financial burden to my parents.

"I'm sure you'll see Sadie your first week at the restaurant. She and her girl squad are fans of our 'close calls.' The regular menu stops at ten. From ten to midnight, we run a limited slider and mini bites menu. It gives the dining room time to finish the final turn and the bar still has food available."

That sounds like a great way to manage kitchen staffing needs too. "That also means the kitchen can fade out stations and move staff to cleaning crew and start sending people home."

His hand hits my shoulder blade. "Told you kitchen life comes back to you. You're already thinking like a gopher."

I can't contain the groan, "I hate that job title. It's not an actual job. You realize that, right?"

"Yep, but it's the perfect description. The one who does a little of everything and works wherever they're needed."

Our old manager nicknamed me 'the gopher' because I was willing to work any job and took any shift without complaints. Now my best friend is bringing it back. *Lucky me.*

When we turn the corner a block from the parking lot, I point to the building across the street. It used to be a boring beige with tons of windows. Now it's dark purple, the shade that's almost black, with a gold sign on the roof. The bottom level is still mostly windows, but they're darkened to the point you can't see in. "What is that? When I was here last, it was still a gym on the bottom floor and a Pilates and yoga studio on the top. I'm assuming the business name is Risqué. But what is it?"

"The bottom floor is a burlesque theater. The top floor is a bookstore and a boutique. Risqué is the name of the theater. Risqué Reads is the bookstore. And Risqué Romance is the boutique. They specialize in sexy apparel and lingerie."

Never in my wildest dreams would I have imagined a burlesque theater in Ridgefield. "What happened to Dog-Eared Pages? That bookstore was awesome. The perfect set up with new books downstairs and used upstairs. The door between the bookstore and Grind House was the perfect way to grab a book and then find a spot to read it. Or even better, pick up a coffee before browsing books."

"That's all still there. The owner of Risqué saw a need for more romance books. Risqué Reads is all romance books, from the super sweet Hallmark movie vibes type stories to the smuttiest smut you'll find in print."

There is something comical about hearing my best friend say smut. He's always been pretty vanilla and would turn bright red when talking about kissing someone. I'm surprised he even knows the word. "Did you really just refer to books as smut?"

"Sexy books. Lots of detail. Sadie refers to them as the type of books you read with one hand." The blush creeps up his cheeks when he says it and he shifts his eyes away from me. Yeah, that's the reaction I expected from my shy, nerdy best friend.

I do not need the visual of anyone reading with one hand. "Dude, I know what it means. I just think it's funny to hear you say it."

When we get to my Expedition, he hands me a set of keys. "You have the address. These are yours. I didn't set the alarm. I'll get a code for you added when I get home tonight. I'm only working until the closing manager gets in at seven. I'll bring home takeout and we can eat while we watch the game. I'll help you with anything heavy once I'm home. Feel free to store your stuff in the garage until you get it unpacked."

"Sounds good. See you tonight."

As I head to Devin's, I pass Risqué and can't help but wonder if that's the answer to the brunette bombshell's clue. Not like I'm planning to go there to find out. But it doesn't hurt to wonder, right?

Chapter 3

After doing hair and makeup for two shows a night the last four nights plus two special events this week, I was ready to crash. Days off are for sleeping in, washing laundry, cleaning the house, and grocery shopping. My housemates and I divided the house into four zones and we rotate who is responsible for each zone weekly, and give one person the week off. This week, the kitchen is mine. Now that I'm done deep cleaning the stove and fridge, I turn my attention to the dishes. Once those are put away, I'll wipe down the counters and I'm done.

I timed everything perfectly. My last load of laundry finishes in time to fold and hang everything before my grocery order arrives. Grocery delivery is the greatest thing ever. My brother is wrong. It doesn't cost me more than going to the store myself because impulse buying is my vice.

Everyone else works on Sundays, so I savor the quiet. Don't get me wrong, I love my roommates. They're the sisters I never had, but sometimes it's nice to have time alone. I unzip my nail kit and choose this week's color combination and stamps. Since I'm working a Rockabilly theme event on Tuesday night, I decide to match my nails to the theme—gray, black, and red with the Rockabilly stamp plate I got in a subscription box a few months ago and never thought I'd use. Once I'm set up, I turn on a movie.

Just as the first coat of polish dries, my phone rings with Devin's ringtone. He's a loud and annoying older brother, so instead of a song, a foghorn blares. I accept the call and leave him on speaker so I can continue working on my manicure. "What's up, chicken butt?"

"The sky," he chuckles. "I know it's your day off, so it's self-care Sunday, but I was hoping I could convince you to come over for dinner tonight. Jameson's been in town a few days now. He trains at the restaurant tomorrow. I thought an impromptu family dinner might be a nice way to welcome him back to town."

"That sounds fun, but I can't. I swiped right and agreed to meet someone for drinks with the possibility of that leading to dinner. If the in-person conversation goes as well as our texts and phone calls, I should be dining at my favorite restaurant tonight."

"How's that possible? Forkn Spoon only serves brunch on Sundays."

I press the stamp against my nail and admire the perfect black polka dot pattern. The gray base color was definitely the perfect choice for this week. "You know what I meant. Raincheck for sure because I don't even remember meeting him."

"What? He was at the restaurant opening."

"With over a hundred other people. I know he went to Ridgefield U, but it's not like you spent a lot of time at the house once you escaped and got your own place with friends. I was three when you started college and five when you moved out." Our almost fifteen-year age difference isn't from a second marriage situation or a miracle baby after years of trying for a second. Not even close. Devin is the planned only child. I am the surprise pregnancy my parents weren't expecting at age forty-five.

"Okay, giggles. Raincheck it is. I'll make sure you officially meet him soon."

Not even my dad calls me by my childhood nickname anymore, but Devin does at least once every time we speak. I stretch my legs out in front of me on the couch and lean against the throw pillow while my nails dry. "What position did you hire him for? I thought you weren't hiring."

"I wasn't officially. I needed someone who could do it all and didn't mind rotating wherever they were needed. When Jameson and I worked together in college, he worked in a position like that. The owner called it the gopher. He'll mostly be in the kitchen on whatever station needs coverage, but a few nights a week, I'll have him behind the bar. He's waited tables before, but I don't think I'll need him to."

"Well, if something comes up and you need front-of-house help on one of my days off, let me know."

"I appreciate it. I'm just walking into Grind House. Want a coffee delivery?"

"Yes, please. Lavender latte and a lemon drop cookie, if they have any. I'm craving tart lemon treats. The half slice of strawberry lemonade cake on Wednesday did not cut it."

"Why only half a slice?"

I let out a frustrated sigh, "Some jackass bought two full cakes plus some. I only got the half slice because a tattoo-covered human statue offered to share with drunk me when I was leaving Pour Me Another."

"This sounds like a story I need to hear about in person. I'll be there in about fifteen minutes unless the line at Grind House is wicked long."

"Wicked? Are you from the East Coast now?" I tease him about his love of this word, but it's all in good fun.

"Hush or I'll bring you a peanut butter mocha instead."

I don't even attempt to hold back the gagging noise. "Disgusting. Peanut butter is gross. It smells weird, and it's sticky. Double yuck. I would lick a sidewalk before drinking that horrible concoction."

"See you soon. We'll drink coffee and catch up."

"Sounds good. My nails will be wet, so let yourself in."

About twenty minutes later, the front door opens and Devin calls out, "It's me."

"I know. I saw you on the security monitor. This grumpy big brother guy demanded we have cameras installed."

He sets the coffee and cookie next to my water glass before plopping onto the oversized chair across from me. "Gotta make sure you nerds are safe." He cocks his head toward the TV. "What are we watching?"

"I just finished *Now You See Me*. I was going to start the second one. Have time to watch it?"

"Sounds good to me. We can watch it after you tell me about this human statue."

I sink further into the couch and close my eyes. "He was gorgeous. A few inches taller than you. Eyes so dark they matched the pupils. This incredible laid-back demeanor. He was leaning against a brick wall, eating my favorite cake straight out of the takeout box. I mentioned being on my way to get a slice and he said his was the last one. Then he told me what happened in line in front of him with someone buying all but one slice. When I pouted, he offered the half he had left. I was a little tipsy and accepted. Mostly because I wanted a reason to be closer to him. Tall, dark, handsome, older. Yes, please."

"So, when do you see him?"

I pop up into a seated position and lean toward him. "I don't. I offered my name and number, but he didn't accept. Something about serendipity, chance meetings, and all that jazz."

After taking a slow sip of his coffee, he smirks. "Let's just hope it doesn't take years, a cross-country move, and both of you engaged to other people for you to find each other again like in that movie."

"What movie?"

"*Serendipity*." The confused look on my face must tell him I have no clue what he's talking about. "John Cusack and Kate Beckinsale, meet cute when buying Christmas gifts in New York. They spend the evening in the city together. She writes her number in a book. He puts his on a five-dollar bill. Each hoping fate will bring them together. Sound familiar at all?"

"Nope!" I reach for the remote and pull up the search. "Adding it to my watch list. This can be my next day off watch."

"So, tell me about your date tonight?"

"Staff writer for the paper, teaches journalism at the community college, and plays guitar in a cover band. He's really nice. Calls when he says he's going to. He's in touch throughout the week. Didn't get all pervy when he found out I work at Risqué." I've never understood the reaction to this. I do hair and makeup for the burlesque shows. It's not like I work at a topless bar.

We relax into a comfortable silence and watch the movie. Halfway through, Devin does his usual big brother thing and heads into the kitchen to make food I didn't ask for but need. He's always had an uncanny way of knowing when I'm not taking care of myself and living off easy meals. He comes back with my favorite comfort dish—Chana Masala, over rice, with a side of spicy cabbage. "Thank you. Just because you're a chef, I don't expect you to cook for me all the time. We could have heated a pizza or something."

He stretches his legs out on the ottoman and settles into the oversized chair. "I enjoy cooking. Especially for you, because you never complain. Plus, I've been doing it all your life. It's second nature at this point."

When we finish lunch, I take our bowls to the kitchen and wash them before he has time to insist that I let him do it. We have about twenty minutes left in the movie, so I don't have enough time to surprise him with his favorite caramel popcorn treat. Instead, I grab two caramel crunch ice cream bars from the freezer. I toss him his before stretching onto the couch. "Thanks, giggles."

When the movie ends, I snag our trash pile from the coffee table. Devin stands and stretches his arms over his head, then he bends at the waist and touches his toes. Once he's upright, he stares at me. "Keep your location on tonight."

I wave my hand quickly, dismissing him. "Yes, dad. Safety 101, someone always knows where you are."

He heads toward the door. "Have fun tonight, giggles. I'll let you know about the raincheck for dinner and meeting Jameson."

Once he's gone, I clean up my nail stuff and get ready for my date. I leave the house excited for a night filled with potential, but thirty minutes later, I'm already home. He checked all the boxes on paper, but paper doesn't show you when someone is a condescending asshole to restaurant and bar staff. The way you treat staff tells me a lot about your character. I finished my drink, paid my tab, and left after my date was rude to the bartender and made inappropriate comments about two of the servers. I couldn't get out of there fast enough.

Chapter 4

The staff at Forkn Spoon have been fantastic. They've welcomed me into the circle and don't mind my grumpy personality or how I keep people at a distance. I see why Devin considers them family. He was right when he said he needed a gopher. He's technically fully staffed, but he needed someone to cover a last-minute day off or call out. Having someone who can work multiple stations in the kitchen or behind the bar has eased things for him. I'm just glad he hasn't asked me to wait tables. That was never my strength.

After two weeks of working five shifts a week in a kitchen, I remember why I told myself to prioritize my self-care. I was ecstatic when I saw there was a local physical therapy center that offered chiropractic care, physical therapy appointments, and massages. Technically, I was discharged from physical therapy but they suggested I do regular check-ins, and honestly, the workout routines a physical therapist put together were always better than something I came up with on my own or got from a personal trainer at a gym. When I contacted the Spine Zone and gave them my medical history, they set up a monthly physical therapy appointment, a chiropractic adjustment, and a massage. The plan also includes a workout calendar for me to do on my own and access to their equipment during the open gym hours. The massage this morning was exactly what I needed after covering the bar last night and to prepare for my weekend shifts. Tonight, I'm covering the kitchen for our kick-ass expediter so she can attend a friend's bachelorette party. Tomorrow I'm back behind the bar. I'm definitely looking forward to my days off on Sunday and Monday. Devin and I are hitting the canyon for a mountain bike ride Sunday morning, and then he planned a cookout with some friends back at the house.

Thirty minutes before the kitchen closes, Travis, our bar manager, enters the kitchen. "Hey, chef. We got an unexpected large group. Normally, I'd say no because the dining room is closed and it's only the close calls menu for a little longer, but it's an emergency."

Devin is technically our chef, but he's already off for the night. We staff the kitchen with three once we move to the close calls menu. After the rest of the kitchen staff clean up their stations, they head out. The 'chef' title defaults to whoever is running the kitchen when Devin's not around. Tonight, that's me. "How is a lack of planning for a group and a request just before midnight an emergency?" I ask as I check three orders before sending them out.

"It's for Brit. She's said the maid of honor dropped the ball and didn't make a reservation for food. She planned a bar crawl without contacting any of the places ahead of time and didn't plan dinner or even appetizers. They haven't eaten. She said it's fifteen of them. Can we do some sliders, chicken strips, and fries? Anything?"

From what I know, Brit has worked here for a few years and Devin considers her family. Not just restaurant family, but extended family because she's friends with Sadie. There's no way I can decline this request. I'm exhausted and half the kitchen is already closed, but I quickly start thinking of ways to make this work.

Luke, our closing line cook, responds before I can, "No problem. There are only three of us, so it won't be anything fancy. Anyone available to cover the table?"

"Kass said she can do it. That leaves me and Kimber behind the bar and Tiff will wait tables in the bar. It's gonna suck, but we'll make it work."

When I helped clean up the vegetable station and prep area, I did a quick count on veggies, so I knew we had plenty prepped. I quickly switch to Spanish and address our dishwasher. Hunter is taking Spanish at the community college. When he found out I was fluent, he asked me to only speak Spanish to him so he could practice. "Hunter, I'm pulling you off the dishwashing station. Help Luke take care of the sliders, chicken strips, and fries. I'll make a couple of family-style salads. If we do trays of sliders, strips, and fries, that is easier than individual orders."

He stares at me blankly, so I repeat myself in Spanish. This time, a bit slower. Maybe right now isn't the ideal time to practice his language skills. Once I repeat the plan in English, he quickly gets to work. "Yes, chef."

Travis slides his phone from his pocket and taps the screen. "I'll let Brit know to head over. I'm going to help Kass set up the table."

Before he leaves, I call out, "Once I'm done with the salads, I'll throw together a mocktail. Sounds like they can use something besides alcohol. We've got some watermelon in the walk-in. I'll puree it with lime and mint, we can top it with sparkling water. What do you think?"

"Pink, bubbly, and fruity. Sounds perfect for a bachelorette party."

I quickly prep three salads—Caesar, Cobb, and spinach. We have some fruit that is about to turn. Instead of throwing it in the freezer, I make a layered fruit salad. The extra hydration will hopefully help with the impending hangovers. Then I work on the watermelon puree. By the time the bachelorette party arrives, the salads and watermelon refresher are on the table, and I'm back in the kitchen. To ease the demand in the kitchen, Travis does a last call for food early, so Luke and Hunter only have the large party to worry about. Once the salads are finished, I call out, "You two finish up the food trays and I'll cover the dishes."

Hunter seems surprised by my offer to wash dishes. "We can switch."

"No, I got it. I know you've been wanting to get more time in the kitchen. I don't mind." Honestly, washing dishes is my least favorite restaurant task, but Hunter is a good kid. I say kid because I'm old enough to be his dad. He'll be nineteen next month. I turn thirty-nine two weeks later.

An hour later, everything in the kitchen is done except the dishes from the bachelorette party table. I'm ready to send Luke and Hunter home, but Luke reminds me I was in two hours before each of them and Travis is the manager on duty tonight, so I'm officially off. I usually leave the restaurant through the back door in the kitchen, but I want to let Travis know I'm leaving, so I head to the bar. Brit runs up to me and wraps her arms around me. "Thank you! I know this threw the kitchen a curveball. I really appreciate it."

"No problem. It wasn't anything fancy, but we'll always make it work when we can for the restaurant family. Luke and Hunter did most of the food prep. I just made salads, then handled clean up and dishes."

"I'm heading in there to thank them now. If this hadn't worked, the only other suggestion was to stand in line for pizza at Slice of Life and bring them in here with us."

"Were we always the last stop on the bar crawl?" I don't remember Devin mentioning that before he left or at our staff meeting this week when he went over any special things coming up. I feel like this is something he would have told us about.

She shrugs with an eye roll. "Not sure. The maid of honor has been really secretive and I swear she's pulling it out of her ass. I think she only mentioned Forkn Spoon because I work here and Sadie's a bridesmaid."

"Sadie? As in Devin's little sister?"

"Yeah, she works with the bride."

I glance toward the table where six or seven of the women are sitting and then scan the bar area, but I don't see anyone who resembles the freckle-faced little girl I remember. "Well, have a good night, Brit. None of you are driving, right?"

"We have rides arranged or live close enough to walk."

"In a group, and no one goes home alone," I state matter-of-factly.

"Yes, *dad*." She teases me about my 'dad personality' a lot. I can't help it. Protecting people and always thinking about safety isn't something I can just shut off because it's not my job anymore. At least I like to think she calls me the restaurant dad because of that and not because I'm old. Most of our kitchen staff are in their early to mid-twenties. Devin offers an apprenticeship through Ridgefield U's culinary program and he's hired most of the staff through that.

When she heads into the kitchen, I get Travis's attention, "I'm heading out. I was in two hours before Luke and Hunter. Are you joining us for the ride on Sunday morning?"

He nods as he loads the empty glassware into the dishwasher. "Yeah, I'll meet you at the trailhead at ten. Thanks again for making this work tonight."

"No problem. Have a good night."

When I leave the restaurant, I walk in front of the window and see the knockout brunette. She's sitting at the corner booth with five people. Her finger taps on the window, and she motions for me to come into the bar. I shake my head and mouth, "Have a good night," before walking to the staff parking behind the building.

Would going inside and talking to her be fun? Of course. But she is far too young for me. She's right where she needs to be, spending a night at a bar with friends her age.

Chapter 5

As soon as I see him, I knock on the window and wave toward the door, hoping he'll join us. Instead, he waves and offers a silent 'Have a good night.' I push my way out of the corner. "I'll be right back. I just saw someone I know."

By the time I make my way through the crowd and out the door, he's gone. I sprint around the corner, thinking maybe he parked in the public lot down across the street, but by the time I get there, I don't see him. *Dammit.*

I spend the next hour making meaningless conversation with the bachelor party who joined us once we finished our late dinner. Their night started at a local card room for a charity poker tournament. I'm sure their last-minute decision to join us was because Katrina sent her fiancé one too many sexy photos. The nice part about him joining us is I am no longer on 'make sure the bride-to-be makes it home' duty so I'm free to head home before last call.

After kicking off my shoes and peeling the skin-tight dress off my body, I face plant onto my bed without bothering to take off my bra and panties. Tonight was both the most fun I've had in ages and a nightmare. Katrina deserved the best bachelorette party ever, but her sister is not a planner. Hailey refused anyone's help, and it was apparent she didn't know she needed to notify the bars about the hop so they could have things ready. And how do you forget to plan food?

Thankfully, Brit got Travis and whoever was working in the kitchen to take care of food for us. My brother seriously owed them all a bonus or something for pulling it off. I can't believe I saw the tattooed human statue for the first time since the day we met while I was blocked in the corner of the booth and couldn't get out fast enough to chase him down. Serendipity is a cruel bitch.

The next morning, I wake to a text from Devin reminding me about the invitation to meet him and some friends for a five-mile mountain bike ride on Sunday morning. There is no way I'm making it to that. No matter how much I love that trail. I'm helping a friend at a hair show in San Francisco today and promised to crash at her place.

Sorry, I promised friends I'd stay in SF tonight. It's been far too long since I've headed that way. I'll be back for the cookout though. Let me know what to bring. BTW whoever closed the kitchen last night were fucking rockstars. We ended up there with a last-minute request because we needed food. Brit talked to Travis and he worked with the kitchen to make it happen. They deserve a bonus or something. I made sure we tipped big time.

Jameson told me about it when he got home. He was going to decline, but Luke and Hunter said they could do it. Travis made sure they got a share of the tip. Jameson refused his cut and said to give it to Kass, Luke, and Hunter.

I didn't realize he was working. I would have introduced myself.

He said similar. Looks like you'll meet him at the cookout. You don't have to bring anything. Maybe make sure you come home from SF with both shoes this time.

Lose a shoe while getting a piggyback ride one time and no one lets you forget it.

What can I say? It's not every day I wake up to a phone call at 3am from a very drunk giggle box. 'Devin, I lost my shoe and now I have to hop because the street's dirty and I don't want my feet on dirty floors.'

I promise. No losing shoes. And no 3am phone calls or texts.

Well, maybe. I can't guarantee drunk-me won't decide you need hilarious photo updates.

Looking forward to them. Have fun tonight and be safe.

After eight hours at the hair show, demonstrating products for Sabrina's new product line, I was ready for a night of fun. The timing for the event couldn't have been better. My favorite band, *Cascade*, was playing at Gracie's, my favorite music venue in San Francisco. What's not to love about an old warehouse turned into a bar featuring live music? Sabrina and I are meeting her roommate, Cora, and some of their friends for the concert. I guess their friend is dating the bar manager, so we have a VIP table. Once we get to the front of the line, we show our IDs and tickets, then head to the bar.

The bartender greets Sabrina by name when we get to the front of the line. "Sabrina, great to see you tonight. What can I get you?"

"Hey, Toby. Give me whatever local beer you have that you recommend. You never steer me wrong. This is my friend Sadie. She hates beer. She's going to want one of Vinny's special off-the-menu cocktails."

Toby pushes his glasses in place. He has that whole bearded hipster vibe going for him and it really works. I can see why Sabrina had totally crushed on him when she was a teenager. They even have one of those pacts where they promise to marry each other if they're still single when she's thirty, and he's thirty-five. "No problem. He's trying out a new infused vodka from our distributor. Do you want grapefruit or strawberry?"

"Is that the only hint I get? What mixers is he using?"

Toby shakes his head as he slides the beer toward Sabrina. "The Irish red. Just tapped it about an hour before we opened. As for the cocktail, Vinny wants feedback. You only get to know the vodka flavor."

"I'll take grapefruit."

He turns to face the tattoo-covered bartender at the other end of the bar. "Vinny, I need a grapefruit special for the VIP table."

"On it!" he replies while he fills two pints of dark beer. Vinny has the stereotypical bartender look go for himself—a simple cotton shirt that fits snugly enough for everyone to know he has a muscular chest, shoulders, and arms, but is loose enough to be comfortable. The shirt is paired with jeans and sneakers. Everything about him screams 'hot bartender' who knows women are staring at him, but I know he only has eyes for his girlfriend. Cami and Vinny had the cutest love story. She's his best friend's little sister and their fake relationship during her brother's wedding celebration led to them realizing they were destined for each other.

"He'll bring it over to you. That will be twelve dollars."

I swat Sabrina's hand when she tries to pay and place a twenty on the bar. "Don't even think you're buying the first round. We're celebrating your success today. Your new line was a hit. You've already sold out."

Toby holds out the money toward me. "In that case, this round is on me. Congrats, Sabrina. Cora told me about the show."

I shove the money in my pocket. "Next round's on me. Don't let her pay."

"No problem."

As we head to the table, I gently hug Sabrina. "I can't believe the perfect timing for my night in the city. An incredible show where my super talented friend launched a new product line and a concert with friends."

"Thanks for your support today. I swear the line did as well as it did because you were so great about explaining what you were using and why you chose certain things."

"It was easy. I've been using the products for the last six months at Risqué. I know them well and everything I said was true."

Once we get to the table, Sabrina and I snag the spots with the best view of the stage, even though we both know we're going to make our way closer once the band's set starts. She quickly reintroduces me to everyone. "Hey, ladies. You all remember Sadie, right?

We went to beauty college together." They nod and greet me. "Sadie, a quick refresh. You know Cora. This is Cami. She's the reason we have the VIP table tonight. And this is Paige."

"Hi, thanks for letting me crash your girls' night."

"No problem," Cami, the curvy brunette with impeccable style, replies. Her long black skirt has a slit up each side. It's something I would wear for a fancy function, not a concert at a bar. But she paired it with a V-neck emerald top that showed off her breasts, making it the perfect concert outfit. "You're always welcome. There was no way Stefan was missing the concert, so it's not just a girls' night. He tagged along with Paige."

The blonde across the table from me laughs. "Husbands. So needy sometimes."

Cami playfully hip-bumps her. "Not like Vinny's much better. He just runs the place, so he uses that as his excuse."

Speaking of the tattoo-covered devil. He squeezes between Cami and Paige and sets a tray of drinks on the table before slipping his arm around Cami's waist. "Talking about me, baby?"

"Mmm hmm," she purrs as he nuzzles his face against her neck. "Thank you for the drinks and reserving the table."

"You're welcome. I would have covered the concert tickets too, but I know none of you would have allowed that."

"They're far too independent for that," a deep voice says. I look over to Paige and see a tall brunette with wide shoulders and muscular arms scoot in next to her. He towers over the table. Even if Sabrina hadn't told me,

I would have assumed he was military, former military, or some sort of protector. "Isn't that right, cupcake?"

"It sure is. I didn't even let my husband buy my ticket tonight."

Vinny laughs as he shakes his head. "Well, you might have paid for your ticket tonight, but the drinks are covered. We heard someone had a fantastic product launch, so round one is on the house. Toby has round two covered. And someone who wants to remain anonymous is covering the rest of the tab."

I try to protest. "I can't let someone pay for me. I'm not really part of the group."

Stephen shakes his head. "Yes, you are. You're friends with Sabrina and have known Cora for years. You're part of the group."

Vinny sets a drink in front of me. "Don't argue. Your money's no good here. This is the cocktail I'm testing tonight. Let me know what you think. I also have a strawberry option if you want to try that later."

I lift the highball glass and twirl it. Then I smell it before taking a sip, followed immediately by a second sip. "This is good. I love the fruit frozen into the ice cubes. I also love that the rim isn't sugared since the drink's not a sweet drink. I know flavored sugar is the hot new thing, but sugar doesn't belong on all drinks."

Vinny whispers something in Cami's ear, causing her to turn beet red. Paige hands her beer to Stefan. "The new Irish red." Then she turns to me. "Vinny and Cami are huge fans of flavored sugar for other uses *besides* cocktails. I'm surprised any of it ends up on the glasses."

Vinny gently smacks Cami's ass. "Let me know when you're ready for another round. I need to get back to the bar. I'm sending Jackie over as soon as she's done getting stuff set up backstage. I told her she didn't have to work tonight, but she insisted on at least making sure the band was taken care of."

"I can't blame her," I remark before taking another sip of my cocktail. "Ashley seems so down to earth and relatable. Her backstage lives before events are always so much fun to watch. She and the guys seem to have a really fun friendship too. Plus, Evan is totally hot."

"You're not heading back to Ridgefield tonight, right?" Cami asks.

"No, tomorrow morning. I have to be at my brother's for something in the afternoon. Why?"

She places her finger against her lips and leans across the table. "Once the crowd clears out, we're hosting the band for an after-party. Vinny's known them for years, since before Ashley took the lead singer spot. The guys want to play poker, and Ash is looking forward to a relaxing night with all of us. You must stay."

There is nothing that would get me to decline that offer. "Hmm, hanging out with my favorite band, why on Earth would I say no to that? Is this one of those leave your phones and other devices in a safe situation, or can I get a few photos and autographs?"

Stefan chuckles. "They will definitely agree to photos and autographs. Paige gets updated photos every time they're in town. There might be more photos on her phone of them than me."

"Not entirely true. But, yes, they're great to their fans and won't mind pictures."

"Fantastic, because my brother is also a huge fan and I'm the bratty little sister who doesn't mind making him jealous."

Cami cackles. "I'm the same way. My brother and his wife aren't in town this weekend, so they're missing out too. I'm definitely sending them pictures."

The house band starts the show with a five-song set to get the crowd warmed up. Then *Cascade* takes the stage. Once the concert ends and the crowd clears out, Vinny and Stefan set up the poker table and I help Cami set up dominoes at another table while everyone else helps with cleaning up. Paige and Sabrina set out a nacho buffet with the slow cookers Vinny and Cami had waiting in their apartment over the bar.

Vinny locks the door and then calls out, "We are officially closed for a private party."

I skip the poker game because I have never understood the game. Instead, I sit at the bar and visit with Ashley, who is just as down-to-earth in person as she seems in her videos. Her husband Cole never takes his eyes off her while he's playing cards. "How long have you and Cole been together?"

"Since I was seventeen. We had some time apart when my gig with the band went from temporary while covering a maternity leave to permanent lead singer. We each casually dated when we were apart, but nothing serious. We just needed some space to figure things out. What about you? Anyone special in your life?"

"Not even close. I was the shy bookworm who convinced her dad to let her graduate from high school early. I never went to school dances or anything like that. It wasn't until about six months into beauty school that

I found my confidence. I casually dated. Had a serious relationship for about nine months. He was older and was ready for the lifetime commitment thing. I wasn't. I was barely nineteen at that point. I'm on every online dating site now."

She gathers her hair to the side and quickly braids it. "So casual is your thing right now. There's nothing wrong with that."

"I'm open to something serious, but it has to be with the right person. There's no point spending time in a commitment if you know you want different things. You know?"

She nods and then glances at Cole. "Exactly why we needed a break. I wanted something he wasn't ready for. Once we were both in the same place, it clicked. I'm a firm believer it happens when it's supposed to and when it does, it happens quickly. That's what happened to Vinny and Cami when they finally got together. Paige and Stefan were the same way."

Those were love stories I knew all about thanks to Sabrina filling me in earlier tonight. "I'm only twenty-three. I have plenty of time."

Ashley clinks her beer glass against my cocktail glass. "Exactly. Enjoy life. You'll find your person when you're supposed to. Now, what do you say we ditch this game night and head upstairs for girls' night? Cami said she has stuff for face masks, manicures, pedicures, and hair masks."

"Sounds perfect." I wiggle my fingers in front of her. "I did my nails yesterday before a friend's bachelorette party. The music theme was perfect because her fiancé is a concert pianist and your show tonight."

She grabs my hand. "You did these?"

"Yeah. I used a nail stamp, but I did it myself."

"These are gorgeous. Any chance you brought stamps?"

"I sure did. Sabrina told me she wanted help with nails while I was in town. She subscribes to a monthly manicure box but hasn't figured out how to use everything."

Ashley hops off the bar stool. "Okay, I'm going to refill my beer and make a nacho plate. Then we are heading upstairs." She stops at the poker table to see Cole, then walks over to where the rest of the girls are playing dominoes. "Who's ready for girls' night?"

"Me!" Cami says as she stands. "I have everything ready. Follow me, ladies. It's beauty night. No boys allowed."

I can see why Sabrina loves this group of friends so much. They're incredibly welcoming and make everyone feel like family. By the end of the night, I feel like I've known everyone for years. Before crawling into the couch bed at Sabrina and Cora's apartment, I send Devin photos from tonight.

> Bucket list item checked off. I met *Cascade*, hung out with Ashley, and got photos with the entire band. I have officially partied like a rockstar with rockstars.

I'm so jealous. I'm sure you had a blast.

I did. And because I'm the nice sibling, I got you signed merch.

You are the sunshine to my grumpy.

Is that a jab at my love of grumpy-sunshine romances?

You know it. If your life was a Romance book, you'd want a grumpy-sunshine, brother's best friend, age gap story.

Sign me up for that. Got any hot friends to introduce me to? Preferably the covered-in-tattoos type.

Nope. Rule number one for my friends is don't date my sister.

Ass.

Goodnight giggles. Sleep well. Let me know when you're on your way home.

Chapter 6

When Devin told me he wanted to have a few people over tonight, I thought it would be the staff from the restaurant and a handful of other guests. Instead, about fifty people are gathered through the common areas of the house and in the backyard. Outside of my coworkers, I only recognize two faces—Dan, my first tattoo artist, and Carlie, my physical therapist. They're seated by the firepit with a few others, so I join them. "Hope you don't mind if I intrude."

Carlie slides to the side, making room for me on the bench. "Not at all. Jameson, do you know everyone?"

"Only you and Dan."

"Everyone knows Dan," Carlie quips.

"He's responsible for my first three tattoos."

She quickly introduces me to the other four people—her fiancé Eric, Dan's niece Poppy, Poppy's husband Dave, and Dean. They're all artists at Dan's shop. The man who's old enough to be my father holds his beer bottle in the air. "Pretty sure most of the guests could say I got them started on their love of tattoos. I've been tattooing as long as you've been alive. Likely longer. Next month is forty years. I've lost track of how many tattoos I've done over the years, but I know I've played a part in at least fifty tattoo careers. How long ago did I do your first tattoo?"

I tap my beer bottle against his. "I'll be thirty-nine in about two months. I got it on my nineteenth birthday."

"Well, be sure to get on my schedule because I officially retire at the end of the year. My crew's staying on and Poppy will run the shop. I'm moving to a silent partner. Skin Deep is remaining a family business." He winks at Poppy.

Poppy pulls her leather jacket closed and zips it. "It's in good hands, Uncle Danny. I promise."

"I know, sweetheart. You've been working there since you were fifteen. It was your dream since you were nine or ten to take over one day and you've done everything I've asked to make it happen. I couldn't pick a better person to hand the keys to in December." Then he shifts his focus to me. "I'm serious about calling the shop. I'd love to do at least one more piece for you."

"I'll call the shop tomorrow. One last tattoo from my favorite artist." I take a long pull from the bottle and my eyes shift to the sliding door just as she steps onto the patio.

She walks over to Devin at the grill and hugs him. When he releases her, he points toward me and calls out. "Hey, Jameson. Come meet Sadie."

What? Cake girl is Sadie?

It takes me a few seconds to rise to my feet. I slowly make my way across the yard and see the exact moment when she realizes it's me. Her eyes narrow and her eyebrows scrunch. "You?"

I jog up the four porch steps. "Me."

"I'm confused. I know I didn't go to a fancy college and I don't know much about mythology, but I'm certain Jameson isn't a mythological creature."

I lean against the porch railing. "Last name."

Devin looks between us as he takes the chicken off the grill and puts it on a tray, then his eyes widen as if he's just put the puzzle together. The tongs clang against the metal tray. "You're the tattooed statue?"

This description makes me chuckle. "Yeah. And she's the girl who stole my cake."

"I did not. You offered half of it. Then I saw you when I was at Forkn Spoon on Friday night. You walked past the window. Why didn't you at least say hi? I tried to catch up with you, but you disappeared. I couldn't figure out where you went."

I set my drink on the railing. "I usually leave through the back door, but I needed to tell Travis something. I exited through the front, then walked to the staff lot behind the building."

Devin scoots between us, holding the tray in one hand. His other hand slams against my shoulder. "Remember the rule."

My head bobs slowly. "You don't have to tell me twice."

When he's at the sliding door, Sadie steps closer to me until there's barely space between us. "That rule is some misogynistic bullshit. I'm an adult. I get to decide who I spend time with, not him."

If there wasn't a railing behind me, I would step backward to give us space, but I can't. I knew she was trouble the moment I saw her, but I didn't realize my attraction to her could cost me my new life. "Sadie, we really shouldn't."

"Why? And don't give me the bullshit about bro code. Tell me you're not available or not interested."

"It's neither of those. I'm too old for you. I work for your brother. I'm living in his guest room. It's too complicated. If things went bad between us, it puts him in an awkward position. I'd feel bad, so I'd leave. I need this new start." I place my hands on the railing and lift myself to sit on it. "I *really* need it."

Sadie steps to the side and then rests her back against the railing next to me. "Devin told me what happened. He let me know you were moving into my room."

"Your room?" That's the first I knew I'd taken her room.

"When he bought the house, he set that room up with the queen-sized bed and furniture in case I moved in. I rent with friends, but he wanted me to know I was welcome here. I usually crash there on nights he has parties and over the holidays. We're big on no drinking and driving. I live within walking distance of downtown, so I don't have to worry when I go out. I'll be sleeping on the couch tonight."

I shake my head. "Nope. He asked me to set up the couch bed in his office in case someone needed it. I have a feeling that it's meant for you."

She hops onto the railing and nudges my shoulder. "How are you adjusting to everything?"

I'm not sure how much Sadie knows about my injury and recovery. But if Devin knows she called me a tattoo-covered statue, it's obvious the two siblings were close. She likely knows I told him I'm unsure if Ridgefield will keep my interest. Small-town life can be boring. College-town life is fun when you're in college, but I'm not sure it's the place for me long-term in my late thirties. "It's good to be busy again. I don't think working at the restaurant is my lifetime goal, but Devin was right. Every day is different, yet also having a routine is good for me. It's nice to not only be needed, but accepted. Sundays and Mondays are the hardest because I'm still figuring out how to occupy my days off."

"Well, I usually have those days off unless I'm working a special event. Let me know if you're ever looking for someone to hike, mountain bike, scuba dive, or snorkel. I'm usually up for anything outdoors, but I also love a good movie binge with snacks. I'm hoping for twenty-five jumps before I turn twenty-five, so skydiving is also an option."

I didn't realize she enjoyed all the outdoor stuff I love. Damn. If only she wasn't my best friend's sister and fifteen years younger than me. I might actually let myself believe there was a chance for us. "My skydiving days ended after the one time your brother and I went in college, but I'm up for the rest. I was just looking at scuba diving and snorkeling options down the central coast. I thought it might be fun to camp and hit the water. Your brother looked at me like I had three heads when I suggested it. It doesn't seem like anyone at the restaurant does either. I figured I'd be on my own."

She swings her legs from side to side. "Don't you remember?"

"Remember what?"

Her head rests against my shoulder. "My hint. Risky and risqué. I'm the one you want to reach out to for outdoor adventures. We should plan something."

Before I can second guess myself, my hand lands on her thigh and gently squeezes. "Is risqué the theater?" I had wondered if that was the answer to the clue since Devin told me about the burlesque theater. I'd even considered going to a show in hopes of seeing her, but the times conflicted with my work schedule. Plus, I kept trying to convince myself it was a bad idea since I'm much too old for her.

"Yeah, I do hair and makeup there Wednesday through Saturday. On Tuesdays, you'll find me at Risqué Reads sometimes as an employee covering for a day off, but mostly as a bookworm who is there for a new release. I also run my hair and makeup studio out of the theater. I have a private entrance. I'm there by appointment for that." She hops off the railing and turns toward me. "What are you doing a week from Sunday?"

"No plans. Why?"

"It should be perfect weather for an underwater adventure. What do you say? Are you up for it? I'll show you my favorite spot?"

I press my lips together, stopping myself from instantly accepting the offer. Two friends hanging out doesn't break my promise to Devin. I need to find people with common interests. Her hands landing on my thighs pull me from my thoughts. "Jameson, I might not agree with it, but I get it. We can just be friends."

The problem is, I don't think I can be *just* friends, but I also know I can't walk away from her. I'm royally screwed.

Chapter 7

B efore locking my car door, I make sure I have everything—camera gear, water, phone, and keys. I'm set for a few hours under the night sky. From telescope watchers to photographers to those enjoying the show without equipment, the canyon is filled with people ready to watch the meteor show. Devin always tells me to be careful and bring a friend. I told my roommates about it, but no one wanted to tag along. I'm not the type to stay home because no one else can join me.

I make my way up the trail to my favorite spot. I'm hoping that since it's one of the furthest lookouts, it won't be as crowded. When I get to the top, I'm disappointed to see someone else already on the bench, but it doesn't look like he has any gear with him. I walk up behind him. "Do you mind if I join you?"

As soon as he turns to face me, my fears subside as I realize it's Jameson. Running into him unexpectedly is a treat. We have plans to visit my favorite dive spot this weekend, but with my busy schedule, this is the only free night I have until then. Jameson slides to one side of the bench, giving me plenty of space to set up. "Hey, Sadie. Of course. This was my favorite spot in college. Far enough from the areas with more benches and picnic tables to not be crowded with families."

"That's why I love it." I quickly unpack my gear and get my camera in place. "No camera or telescope?"

He shakes his head, "No. The fanciest I get for pictures is on my phone. I don't think I've used a telescope since my astronomy class freshman year. What about you? Hobby or something more?"

"Photography has been a passion since I was about seven. Probably something I could make money at if I spent time taking classes. I thought about it, but I was afraid I'd twist something I love into something I don't recognize just because it made me money. Sometimes hobbies should stay hobbies. You know?"

"Can't say I've ever found something I was passionate about like that, but I understand what you mean. I guess in a way I was like that with languages. Grew up in a bilingual English and Spanish house. My high school offered Spanish, Russian, and French. I chose Russian because I wanted to learn something new, and the French teacher was kooky. I continued studying Russian in college. My aptitude scores in the military set me on the path for language study and counterintelligence."

I snap a few photos to test my settings, "Wow. That's impressive. What did you study in Monterey?"

"Arabic. I don't have a ton of use for it in civilian life, but–" his words trail off and he leaves the statement unfinished.

I want to know more about him, but I can tell this isn't something he wants to talk about. I remember Devin telling me about Jameson's deployments to the Middle East and how he did something in Intelligence, but he didn't know many details. There were a few years when I helped my brother pack care packages for the holidays. We always sent a few for Jameson and extra for him to give to friends who didn't receive much. "I always wished we spoke a second language in our house. I took one year of sign language in high school. I was going to do a second, but then I finished school early."

Jameson pops the lid off his canteen and takes a sip before glancing at me. "It's never too late. I happen to know there's not only a great university in Ridgefield, but there's a community college. And you don't have to take classes with the goal of a degree. Sometimes it's fun to take a class just because."

I settle onto the bench and fold my legs crisscross. "I hated everything about high school. The thought of going back into a traditional classroom has zero appeal. I'm sure that seems bonkers to someone with as much training and education as you, but it's just not my thing."

While I can't seem to take my eyes off him, he keeps his focus on the canyon. "There's nothing wrong with that. You found something you love. At the end of the day, all that matters is you're happy. Are you happy, Sadie?"

It wasn't often that my lack of formal education was accepted. The downside to living in a college town was everyone's life revolved around the university schedule. Most of my friends growing up had parents who worked at the university or community college. My mom was a librarian at the community college and my dad worked in Ridgefield U's admission department. It was always assumed Devin and I would both go to Ridgefield. I'm sure my lack of desire to even finish high school disappointed my parents. My dad came to accept it and loves that I found a career I'm passionate about. I haven't spoken to my mom in years. The last time I did she made it clear beauty college wasn't real college. "Yeah, I'm happy. I love what I do. I love the people I work with. Special events keep it interesting and help keep things from getting boring. I can't stand being bored."

"Sounds familiar." He points to the east. "There. It's starting."

We sit in a comfortable silence and enjoy the show. I capture incredible photos thanks to Jameson pointing to meteors throughout the sky. An hour into the show, I wish I had brought food. My toxic trait is staying so busy I forget to eat. I never realize I'm hungry until I sit and relax for a bit. I take a few sips of water, hoping it will satisfy the hunger pangs for a bit.

Jameson reaches under the bench and pulls out a takeout bag from Forkn Spoon. "Did you eat before hiking up here?"

"No. I came straight from work. I'll eat when I get home."

He opens the takeout box, tears off the lid, and loads half the salad greens into it. He places a fork in it and holds it out to me. "Strawberry fields salad with balsamic. I added blueberries, feta, and candied pecans."

I shake my head. "I can't take half your dinner."

He sets the salad on my lap. "Yes, you can. You need to eat, Sadie. If you're a good girl and finish your salad, I'll share my dessert with you." He motions toward the pink box in the bag. "It's Thursday, no lemonade cake, but the chocolate whiskey with caramel frosting is incredible."

Good girl? Did he really just say that? Serendipity is a cruel bitch. Of course, I meet a guy who can slip that into a conversation nonchalantly and who makes every fiber of my being feel alive for the first time, and he's not interested in anything but friendship.

"That's my second favorite cake." I gather the onions onto my fork and drop them back into his salad. "I don't eat raw onion. Those are yours. Thanks for dinner."

"You're welcome."

We continue to watch the meteor shower in silence while we eat. Once I finish dinner, I ask, "Are you enjoying being back in Ridgefield?"

He finishes his last few bites of salad before responding. "Yeah, I am. It's better than I expected. Everyone at the restaurant is great. Devin has a good crew. I'm finding a routine and figuring out life again."

"Do you think the restaurant industry is your future?"

He shakes his head. "I'm right where I need to be now, but it's not something I want to do for the next decade. I have no clue where I'll end up. Until I do, I'm sticking around Ridgefield and working for Devin."

I can't imagine having the career I worked so hard for basically ripped away from me. That must be incredibly difficult. Hair stylist and makeup artist for special events and theater productions isn't at all the same thing as the time and commitment Jameson put into his career and the commitment he made to the military. Devin told me the only thing Jameson ever wanted was a military career, and he'd planned for it since his sophomore year in high school. "I hope it's okay Devin told me a bit about what happened."

"Yeah, sunshine. It's fine. He asked before he shared. It's not anything I hide. Fluke training accident. Someone didn't time things correctly, and I paid the price." He opens the cake box, scoops half onto his empty salad container, and then hands me the container. "I can tell you're holding something back. You can ask me anything."

"If you could do anything, besides being a Marine, what would you pick?"

"My backup plan was always something in law enforcement. But I can't pass the physical."

"And your background is in languages and boots-on-the-ground support, right?" I don't understand what 'boots-on-the-ground' meant, but it's how Devin described Jameson's job whenever I asked.

He turns slightly to face me. "And web security, secured communications, that sort of thing. Why? I can practically see the wheels turning. What are you up to?"

I turn slightly away from him to get shots of the opposite side of the canyon. "Nothing. Can't a girl spend time getting to know her brother's best friend? Aren't you the one who said we could be friends?"

"You're a horrible liar. I'll let you have your secret for now, but promise to clue me in someday?"

"Deal."

It's not like I have details right now. I'm not sure if the idea I have will even work, but it's worth finding out. The first thing on my to-do list tomorrow is calling Paige's husband, Stefan. He's ex-military and works for a private contract company that specializes in secured communications and web security. If anyone has connections that might have an option for Jameson to get back into the career he obviously loves, it's Stefan.

Chapter 8

I pull my bike off the rack, then lock my Expedition. A morning trail ride is always my favorite way to start my day off. As I start up the trail, I hear a familiar voice behind me, "Jameson, are you following me?"

I don't need to look to know it's Sadie. I stop and wait for her to catch up. "What can I say? This seems to be a favorite place for both of us. Last night, you said you had to work today. Did your plans change?"

She stops her bike next to mine. "No. I don't have to be in for a couple of hours. I figured I'd spend a little time on the trail. I'd love to do a five or six-mile ride today, but I don't have time. I'm going to do the easy two-mile." She points to the purple pouch on her handlebars. "I packed my camera, hoping to have enough time for a few photos, but the focus is on getting in some exercise. I'm not sure why there are three gyms in town when we have so many trails to explore." She secures her helmet and then tugs on her gloves. "What about you? Which trail are you doing?"

"I have all day, so I was planning on the six miles." I glance toward the two-mile trailhead. "Unless—"

She smirks as she pushes herself back on her seat and heads toward the trail. "Unless you want to do a two-mile warm-up." She pedals forward before glancing over her shoulder. "I'll race you. The first one back at their car wins. Loser buys snacks for our dive trip."

"Oh, princess. I'm incredibly competitive. It's a deal."

She pedals faster and leads me down the path. The two-mile trail is a relatively flat loop that is marked for one-direction traffic since it's narrow compared to the other trails. The downside to this is it's virtually impossible to pass her. She increases her speed and stands on her pedals, leaning forward slightly, giving me a magnificent view of her ass. This woman is trouble with a capital T and the way she winks at me over her shoulder as she pushes her ass out tells me she knows it.

When we get back to the parking lot, I watch as she loads her bike onto the rack. I offer to help, but she refuses. Once her door opens, I offer a friendly, "Have a good day, Sadie. Thanks for the warm-up ride," before heading toward the six-mile loop.

"See you later, Jameson. Hopefully, you enjoyed the view. Oops, I mean ride. Enjoy the six-miler." Her door slams shut before I can respond.

After my ride, I head home to shower. I still have a few hours before my tattoo consult with Dan. I have an appointment with him next month. He wants to meet today to look at the space I have on my back and my thigh to figure out the best option for the detailed piece I described at the barbecue. My current pieces tell my life story. I've documented my education, my travels, and my hobbies. The one thing I haven't done is honor my family. I want something to represent my parents and siblings that also incorporates our ties to Mexico.

I showed Dan a photo of my great-grandparents' home in Mexico City and the tree at my parents' house, where we took our annual birthday photos. I mentioned wanting to add a few details, like stacks of books to represent my bookworm sisters and a soccer ball for my brother. Maybe a wine glass for my mom and since I got my love of outdoor adventure from my dad, I knew I needed a mountain bike included. I feared I had too many ideas and not enough space, so Dan and I agreed to a brainstorming session today and then he'd work on a few sketches. We'll meet again a couple of weeks before my appointment.

It's a beautiful day and midday parking downtown can be difficult, so I decide to walk. I leave with more than enough time to get to Dan's shop. I kill some time by birthday shopping for my sisters. I head into Dog-Eared Pages and stand in line. I have a list of titles and authors from each of them, but no clue where to start looking. When I get to the front of the line, I set my phone on the counter and slide it toward the cashier. "Can you tell me where I can find these books?"

The petite gray-haired woman who looks old enough to be my grandmother nods, "We have the first two in stock in the Young Adult Fantasy section. It's alphabetical by author. You'll find the others in the Romance section. They're adult, not YA. Are these gifts for someone special?"

"My sisters. Their birthdays are in a few weeks."

She slides my phone back to me. "Buy the first two from us. Then head over to Risqué Reads. One of their employees does incredible custom one-of-a-kind watercolor painted edges. If they don't have anything in stock, you can order any book. The turnaround time is usually ten to fourteen days at this time of year. The wait is anywhere from ten to twelve weeks before the holidays."

I didn't even know painted edges were possible. That definitely sounds like something both of my sisters would enjoy. "Thank you. I'll head there next."

Once I buy the fantasy books, I make my way to Risqué Reads. I pull open the door and am greeted by a familiar face. Sadie is sitting on the stool behind the cashier's counter. "Now you really are following me."

I glance around the small shop. It can't be over fifteen-hundred square feet, but it doesn't feel small. The shelves are labeled by trope. There's a window bench and two chairs at the back of the store down two steps. It appears to be set up to encourage customers to relax in the store. The small tables and shorter shelves throughout the shop display coffee mugs, water bottles, socks, bookmarks, and other gifts. "It's not Tuesday. I didn't expect to find you here. I figured when you said you were working this afternoon, it was for the theater."

"Just covering for a few hours. What can I help you find? Maybe a best friend's little sister, age gap romance." She points toward the shelf to my left labeled 'Yes, Daddy.' "Or maybe a Dom Daddy story."

I grab two water bottles to add to the birthday boxes I'm sending my sisters. 'A Book a Day Keeps Reality Away' and 'A Day Without Reading Is Like . . . Just Kidding. I Have No Idea.' are perfect for them. I set them on the counter in front of Sadie. "I'm looking for four books. Two for each sister. The clerk at Dog-Eared sent me over here to ask about the watercolor edges."

"We have about twenty in stock and the artist can customize any book. There's no one on the waiting list right now. You'd be next. What books are you looking for?"

"These," I say as I show her the list.

"Oh, they have good taste. And you're in luck. We have all four in stock. I only have one with watercolor edges. You'll have to order the other three. And if you want, you can customize the edges with any design. In the one we have, the male lead calls the female lead cupcake, so the edges are cupcakes. If you think your sister would want something that represents her tastes, the artist can do that."

Until ten minutes ago, I didn't even know this was an option. Trying to decide what they would want feels overwhelming. "What would you want? I don't know how to decide this."

"I have a lot of decorated edges. Benefits of the artist being one of my roommates. I like the edges to represent the book. I've read these. Do you want me to help you?"

I dig through the basket filled with hilarious book quotes and nod. "Yes, please. Whatever you think they'd like works for me."

She quickly fills out the order form and turns the tablet toward me. "This is your total cost, including purchasing the books. Is this okay?"

I pull my wallet from my pocket. "That's it? Just under one-hundred dollars doesn't seem like enough."

"The books are paperback, so that helps keep it low. Plus, you're buying more than two decorated edges, so you get a discount. The cost of the books, plus fifty percent of the artist's fee, is due today."

"I'll pay it all. Will the store call me when they're ready?"

She sets the tablet in front of me. "Yes. As soon as they're ready, someone will call. Just fill in the contact info and you're all set. Can I help you find anything else or just the four custom books, two water bottles, stickers, and the bookmarks?"

I look at the small pile I've accumulated in front of me. "What bookmarks? I didn't look at bookmarks."

"Just seeing if you were paying attention. You've hardly looked at me since walking into the store. The first day we met, you couldn't take your eyes off me. But ever since then, you've barely made eye contact."

Damn. I was hoping she hadn't noticed that. I shift on my feet as I pull cash from my wallet. Once I set the exact change on the counter, I raise my eyes from the pile of gifts to meet her caramel eyes. "It takes all my self-control to behave around you. I don't just want to stare at you. I want to touch you, to kiss you, to pull you onto my lap. But I can't do any of that. It's not appropriate."

She finishes wrapping the water bottles in tissue paper and places them in the bag. "Because of my brother."

I shake my head. "No. I've always thought 'bro code' was bullshit. You're too young. I'm in a period of transition. I'm feeling lost. The last thing I need to do is pull someone into my shit. Especially when I know this is a temporary stop for me. That's not fair to you."

She drops the stickers into an envelope and adds it to the bag. "Hey, Jameson. Before you decide what is or isn't fair to me, maybe ask me. I'm not looking for wedding vows and baby strollers. Temporary can be fun." She holds out the bag to me. "Think about it."

Oh, sunshine. I have thought about it. Probably more often than I should. I accept the bag and pretend not to notice when her fingers linger on mine.

Chapter 9

Forkn Spoon is packed when Olivia and I arrive. Thursday nights during the school year are busy everywhere. The pre-weekend celebration for everyone without Friday classes is popular. Those with classes on Fridays still enjoy the night. They just head home early. When my friend Abigail asked if I wanted to meet up tonight before she headed back to Chicago, I knew our only chance of getting a table to ourselves was to head to Devin's restaurant. Being the owner's baby sister has perks. The 'no reservations in the bar area' rule doesn't apply to me. When I called this afternoon, Kimber said he'd toss a reserved sign on my favorite booth before he left and let the closing bar staff know it was for me.

Olivia and I weave through the shoulder-to-shoulder crowd of college students as we head to the table by the window. Once I slide into the booth, I glance at the drinks special on the board by the bar. "I've lived here all my life and somehow I still manage to forget how chaotic Thursday nights get."

Olivia drums her fingers in beat to the music while she scans the menu. "It's been a decade and a half for me, and I'm still not used to it. Thanks for inviting me to tag along tonight. I didn't feel like being home alone."

"No problem. You're going to love Abby, well Abigail, unless she tells you differently. We've known each other *forever*. She's always been Abby to me."

"Probably the same way I'm still Livvy to certain people back in Kansas."

Olivia and I met a few years ago when the owners of Risqué wanted to utilize the two commercial spaces over the theater. The owners knew Olivia from her years working at Grind House and Dog Eared Pages. I had seen Olivia around town for years, but she's a little older than me, and we didn't have much in common. Or I didn't realize we had things in common. When they convinced Olivia to open Risqué Reads, we discovered our similarities.

Last year, when her marriage ended, a few of us moved in to help her keep her house. She needed it as collateral for her business loan. Instead of paying a faceless landlord, we pay a friend. It quickly became more than a roommate situation. The five of us became family. Especially when Belinda and Alexis asked to rent the apartment space. They were my mentors when I was in beauty college and introduced me to theater life. They're more than my bosses and mentors now. They're surrogate moms. Something I didn't realize I missed until I found myself confiding in them the way I knew people did with their mom. Not that I'd ever experienced that.

Tiff bounces over to our table with two drinks in hand. "Travis sent me over with these. He said if you don't like them, he'll make you something else. He doesn't know who Abigail is, so he isn't sure what she wants. Once she gets here, let me know and I'll get it. And I can switch these for whatever you want if you don't like them." She sets a light pink drink in front of Olivia and a blended drink that looks like a frozen coffee in front of me. "Pretty in Pink mocktail for Olivia. It's watermelon and cranberry. Sounds like a weird combo, but it's delicious. Travis just put it on the menu earlier this week. And a mudslide for Sadie. Would you like to order food before the kitchen is slammed again?"

Olivia nods as she sips her drink. "This is fantastic. Tell him thank you. He makes the best mocktails. As for food, I need something greasy and cheesy I'm thinking mozzarella sticks. The large order."

"And nachos, beans, no meat, with guacamole and sour cream. Tell my brother not to go stingy on the sour cream this time. If he has any of that salsa verde, I'll take that on the side. If there's only pico, I'll pass because raw onions are nasty."

Tiff chuckles as she adds the details to our order. "I'm putting your request in word for word. I can't wait to hear about the reaction from the kitchen. The new system not only prints out tickets, it also reads them. Devin can choose the voice, and someone keeps changing the voice when Devin's not around. I walked in yesterday and it was William Shatner, which made us all laugh, except for Devin."

"That's hilarious. Someone should find out if Morgan Freeman is an option."

Just then, Abigail slides onto the bench next to me. "Hi! Oh, my word. This place is wild tonight. It took me ages to get through the crowd. I'm glad you ordered drinks already." Without asking for permission, she steals a sip of mine. "I want whatever this is, please. And I'm starving, so please tell me we're getting food."

Tiff nods. "Yep. So far, a large order of mozzarella sticks and nachos with beans, no meat, guac, and 'don't go stingy on the sour cream.' What else can I get you?"

Abigail scans the bar menu. "Since we've already got a cheese theme going, how about the brie and honey crostini?"

I cock my head toward Olivia. "See? I told you so. You and Abigail are going to get along great."

"Oh no. Did you think we wouldn't? And here I am, so hungry I didn't even introduce myself. I'm Abigail. You must be Olivia, the awesome roommate who owns a bookstore. By the way, I stopped by yesterday and fell in love. It's great."

Tiff interrupts. "I got your appetizers in and the mudslide. Anything else? Otherwise, I'm going to check on my other tables."

I hand her my card. "We're good. Go ahead and open a tab. And you don't have to check in. If we need anything, we'll head up to the bar."

After sliding my card, she returns it to me. "Thank you. Flag me down if you need anything. I'll be back with food when it's ready."

A few minutes later, Travis sets down Abigail's drink before sliding onto the bench next to Olivia. "I'm crashing girls' night and I'm not sorry about it. I have a mandatory meal break and it's ridiculous in here tonight. I will probably have to hop back behind the bar, but my food was ready, so I'm going to inhale this. Help yourself to fries, I will hardly touch them." He motions to the plate with a toasted sandwich and a side of fries. Then he looks across the table at Abigail. "I'm Travis, by the way. And you must be Abigail."

"I'm Abigail." She snags a few fries. "I will take you up on the fries."

Tavis turns toward Olivia. "Have you eaten today?"

"Does a handful of gummy bears count?"

"Definitely not." He slices one half of his sandwich into two pieces and holds it out to her. "Toasted Caprese with pesto instead of mayo."

"That is my favorite, but I'm not taking your dinner."

He leans in and presses his mouth against her ear. Whatever he says is inaudible, but she no longer argues.

Abigail's scrunched eyebrows tell me she's wondering what's going on. I whisper, "Your guess is as good as mine."

After finishing the food Travis had practically forced on her, Olivia smiles. "I know what I forgot to tell you. When my brother was here to visit, aka check up on how I was doing on my divorce anniversary, he set up a profile for me on one of those match sites for one-night stands. He told me everyone needs a hoe phase, and it's time for mine."

"The hoe phase is overrated," I say before sipping my drink.

Travis's gaze shifts from his meal to Olivia. "No one *needs* one, but there's nothing wrong with wanting one. And if you do, you're sitting in a roomful of men who are likely looking for a hookup."

She nudges him before sticking her tongue out at him. "Been there. Done that. And it's not something I want to do again. It's also not something I told Jacob about. He assumed I spent the last year alone."

Travis wipes his hands on his napkin, then whispers something to Olivia that causes her entire face to redden. He doesn't say a word to me or Abigail when he heads back to the bar. Olivia slides his plate in front of her and eats the other quarter of the sandwich he left. "Someone else can eat the fries."

I fold over the table. "Oh no. You two don't get to share secrets like that in front of us and then silently eat his food like nothing happened. Spill it."

Abigail laughs as she looks at Olivia, then across the bar at Travis. "I think I know. They have a friends-with-benefits thing going. Or they did at one point."

"*Did*. Now we're just friends."

Before we can get more details, Tiff brings our food. "Sorry it took so long. The new server stacked tickets. Your three appetizers ended up behind a massive line of orders. How are you doing with drinks? And how did you get fries?"

"I think we're good on drinks." Olivia points to Travis. "He needed a place to sit while he took his break. We charged him."

Once Tiff walks away, Olivia surprises me when she continues to give details without us asking. "Long story short. I married my high school sweetheart. He was the only one I'd ever been with. When I was ready to date, I didn't know what to do because I knew the first few times that I was with someone would be emotional. I asked Travis to be the first, hoping that choosing a friend who doesn't do relationships would be a good experience. I needed to know we wouldn't get attached. And I wouldn't feel like a fool if I panicked and couldn't do it. He was the perfect choice. We're definitely not each other's happily ever after, but he gave me what I needed. Now, enough about me. Abigail, how long are you back in Ridgefield?"

"For a few days, then I head back to Chicago to finish up a work project and pack my stuff because I just accepted the Director position at the museum."

I lunge toward her and wrap my arms around her. "I'm so excited. You're moving home. Where are you going to live?"

"No clue. I'll figure it out though. There's always my childhood bedroom as a temporary option."

The three of us spend the next hour talking and laughing. When I hear last call, I'm surprised to hear Jameson's voice, not Travis's. In the chaos tonight, I didn't notice he was the second bartender. I pile our plates on top of each other, then add our empty glasses. "I'm going to drop off these at the bar while I close out our tab. Then I'll meet you outside."

As I approach the bar, Jameson smiles at me. "Hey, Sadie. Did you and your friends have fun tonight?"

"We did. It was so busy tonight I didn't even notice you were working. If I had, I would have introduced you to Olivia. She's the one I walked in with. She's one of my roommates, owns Risqué Reads, and is the artist who does the custom edges. Abigail is my childhood friend. She lives in Chicago right now, but she's moving back." Once I finish spitting out their biographies, I'm a little embarrassed that I told him all that, since he didn't need to know any of it.

He takes the plates and glasses from me and slides me my receipt. "I got your tab closed out. You're all set."

I hand him the cash tip Olivia gave me and tuck the rest of her share of the tab into my pocket. Neither of us accepted Abigail's money tonight. We told her it was our treat to celebrate her new job. "Good night, Jameson."

"Night, Sadie."

When I join my friends outside, Olivia doesn't even let the door shut behind me before she bombards me with questions. "Who's the new bartender? And why can I feel the attraction between the two of you from out here? You've been holding out on me."

"That's Jameson., my brother's best friend. The one who just moved back to town. He's also the tattoo-covered statue I told you about."

Abigail laughs as she skips down the street. "I need all the details about that, Sadie."

While we walk home, I bring them to speed about the day I met Jameson, how serendipity is a cruel bitch, and how it's going to take all of my self-control not to throw myself at him on our upcoming dive trip.

Chapter 10

Sadie may not have noticed me behind the bar tonight, but I spotted her as soon as she walked in the door. I was busy the entire night, so that helped keep me behind the bar, even though all I wanted to do was talk to her. When Travis took his meal break, I was jealous of the time he got at her table, even though his focus was on Olivia. They appear to have a great friendship. I've seen them around town together a few times. I mistakenly assumed they were dating, and Travis quickly corrected me. They've known each other since she first moved to town. Back then, they both worked at Grind House.

Once the glassware is loaded in the dishwasher, I carry the dirty dish bin through the bar area, checking for anything else that needs to be washed. Then I take it to Hunter. Our Spanish practice is paying off. He understands over half of what I say the first time, and he attempts to use Spanish more frequently. "This is everything from the bar."

Without hesitation, he responds in Spanglish that is an even 50-50 mix of the two languages. "Thanks, man. How was it? You don't do many shifts behind the bar and tonight was non-stop."

"I'll take a busy night over a slow one any day. But I prefer the solitude the kitchen provides versus the bar. And from now on, I need to convince someone I shouldn't work on college night or whatever this was."

Devin chucks a roll at me. His years working in restaurants combined with three semesters studying the language at Ridgefield U means he understands most of what's spoken around him. If he practiced, he could speak Spanish with more confidence. But instead of trying, he typically responds in English. "It's a university town. Every night is college night."

I catch the roll. "Did this touch the floor or trash can?"

"Nope. It's all yours. Don't think I didn't notice you skipped your meal break."

"Travis didn't take his full one either." I tear a chunk of bread off and pop it into my mouth. The soft, fluffy bread practically melts against my tongue. "Have you ever considered doing these as bite-sized and stuffing them with cheese and basting them with melted butter and garlic? Ground sausage could be good too."

Devin wipes down the prep station. "That's a fantastic idea. I'll play around with it. I like both ideas for filling. We can have them at our next staff meeting, if the feedback is good, we'll try them as a special."

I spend the next hour cleaning the bar while Travis closes out the cash registers, runs the end-of-night reports, and splits the tips for bar staff.

When Devin and I get home, we each head to our side of the house to shower and change. A half-hour later, I find him sitting on the sofa, flipping through movie options. He looks over at me. "Is it just me, or does it happen to you? No matter how tired I am when I leave work, I can't go straight to bed. I need a couple of hours to zone out before I sleep."

I sit on the chair across the room and stretch my legs out on the ottoman before opening my book. "Not just you. I'll read for an hour, maybe two. Then when I crawl into bed, I'll stare at the ceiling for another hour before finally seeing the inside of my eyelids."

He grunts a non-response and continues scrolling through movie options. I shift my attention to the latest true crime novel that grabbed my attention. A few minutes later, my eyes haven't left the pages of my book, but I feel his gaze. "What's up, Devin?"

"Just trying to decide if I'm going to say it or stay silent."

"Is it about work?"

"No."

"Is it about something here at the house? Have I broken a house rule or done something to offend you?"

"Not yet."

That tells me it's about Sadie. "Then keep your mouth shut unless you want my opinion."

"She's my baby sister. Don't do anything to hurt her."

I finally look at him. "The last thing I want to do is hurt her. We've run into each other a few times. We have a ton in common. She offered to show me her favorite place to dive. We're just friends. Not even sure we know each other well enough to call her that."

My best friend doesn't say anything after that. He starts his Jim Carrey comedy. Since the actor's face isn't green, I know it's not *The Mask*, but other than that, I have no clue what Devin's watching. I'm not much of a movie watcher. I finish two chapters before I walk to my room. As soon as I collapse onto the bed, my eyes fixate on the ceiling. Thoughts ping-pong from one side of my mind to the other as I debate whether this dive trip is a good idea. The only thing I know for sure is that I want to spend time with Sadie. I toss and turn for two hours while my internal dilemma consumes me.

I want to spend time with her, but I shouldn't because I'm too old.

She deserves someone who is settled.

My life is chaos right now. Everything is up in the air. I don't know where I'll be in three or six months.

She completely captivates my attention in a way no one else ever has. I want to be near her. I know I shouldn't.

Finally, the only thing I can do to settle the internal monologue is to eliminate temptation. I grab my phone from the nightstand and open the hotel reservation. When I booked the room, I got one with two beds. Being that close to Sadie isn't a good idea. I add a second room, then return the phone to the charger. I roll onto my side and pull a blanket over my head. My mind quiets and my eyelids close. Sleep overtakes me.

.

Chapter 11

My dive gear and overnight bag with extra clothes are piled by the door when Jameson arrives to pick me up. We decided to head out this evening instead of the crack of dawn tomorrow. He worked the lunch shift at the restaurant and I finished at Risqué a little after four. I suggested a camping trip for a couple of nights to make the most of the nice weather, since we were driving three hours to my favorite dive spot. When Jameson said he'd take care of the overnight reservations, I expected him to book the campground I told him about. Instead, he found a hotel and got two rooms. Yes, two *rooms.* Not a room with two beds. Okay, I get it. Friend zone for life, but that doesn't mean a girl can't dream. And boy have I. I've had the most intense and detailed dreams I've ever experienced.

I'm throwing together some road snacks when there's a tap on the screen door. "It's me."

"Hey, it's open. Come in."

He stops to wipe his shoes on the mat before stepping into the house. When he sees my pile of gear and bags, he immediately grabs the heavy dive items. "I'll get this into my Expedition. Then I'll come back for the rest."

"Thank you. I'm almost done. Just packing snacks."

"I have some too. And a variety of drinks."

I leave a note on the fridge for my housemates, reminding them where I'll be for the next couple of days. We all have different schedules, so it's not uncommon to go a day or two without seeing everyone, but we let each other know when we won't be home at all.

Jameson is waiting by the passenger side door when I get to the driveway. He takes the soft-sided cooler bag from my shoulder and opens the door. "Do we need to stop for anything?"

"Nope. Not unless you need something." I climb into the front seat and laugh when I see a pink takeout box on the dashboard. "Is the road trip snack you packed cake?"

"Strawberry lemonade with two forks. Buckle up, sunshine."

As soon as I'm buckled, he shuts the door. Then he drops the cooler onto the floor of the back seat where I can reach from my spot. Once we're on the road, we easily fall into conversation.

"How was your day? You said you were doing hair for a special event at the theater."

"We usually have two evening shows, but a few times a month, we do a midday family show. Similar performance style but more clothing. Full costume instead of things that look like lingerie. I like working those events because it gives me a Saturday night off. Not that I work super late on Saturdays anyway. I'm usually done by eight, no later than nine. Our second show starts at nine, so no one needs me after that."

I reach into the cooler bag and pull out the veggie tray with hummus. When I was planning easy snacks, I remembered he ate a lot of hummus at the cookout last weekend. "Did you eat dinner yet?"

"No. It was too early. I grabbed a couple sandwiches from the deli across from Slice of Life. I wasn't sure what you liked, so I got a few options—Mediterranean veggie, Caprese with basil pesto, and falafel. I got tzatziki and tahini sauce on the side for the falafel, so there are options."

I don't remember telling him I'm a vegetarian and I doubt he'd ask my brother, but maybe Devin mentioned it. "I like all of those. The correct answer about the sauce is both."

"My thoughts exactly."

"What about you? Did you get yourself some meat monstrosity? I notice they're all vegetarian options. I'm assuming Devin told you."

Leaving one hand on the wheel, the other reaches across and lands on my thigh. "No, I like all the options I bought, so I'm good. And no one told me, I noticed. Devin keeps chipotle black bean burgers in the freezer. Everything in the pantry basket marked 'Sadie's don't touch' is vegetarian. Plus, each weekly special at the restaurant has a vegetarian counterpart. At the party, you skipped the chicken and burgers. You filled your plate with salad, veggies, hummus, fruit, and two cupcakes. I'm assuming, like me, you couldn't decide between the options and went with one of each."

"For someone who isn't interested in anything more than friendship, you sure notice a lot about me."

His hand squeezes my thigh, and he lets out a long exhalation. "I never said I wasn't interested. I said I couldn't risk losing everything. Those are two very different things, sunshine."

I shift slightly in my seat so I'm staring at him instead of out the front window. "That's twice you've called me that. Why? Is it your default for any woman in your life the way 'babe' is for most guys?"

He turns his head, so his dark eyes lock on mine. "Nope. Just you. Because you brighten my day."

Be still my Romance reading heart. I brighten his day. That is some serious book boyfriend talk right there. I've never been so thankful for bumper-to-bumper traffic heading into the Bay Area in my life. Being stopped on the freeway gives me a chance to do something I've wanted to do since the first time I saw him. I loosen my seatbelt chest strap enough so I can lean across the front seat. I intend for the kiss to be short and sweet, but once I feel his lips against mine, I can't stop. Thankfully, the reaction is mutual. He leans into the kiss, demanding more.

When we part, he laces his fingers with mine before raising my hand to his lips. "Maybe we forget the rule for a few nights and spend this time seeing if this is more than a physical attraction. I think we owe ourselves that and we should do it out of your brother's watchful eye. We've hardly spent any time together, but from the day I saw you dancing on the sidewalk, I haven't been able to get you out of my mind. I knew before I talked to you that you were someone special. I'm not even sure how to describe what I felt that day."

"Lightning bolt. It hit me too. As soon as I saw you, it was like I knew we were supposed to be together. From now until we get home on Tuesday, we'll give this a real chance and get to know each other. Then when we get home, we'll decide if it was a few days of fun or something more."

We spend the next two hours eating our car picnic, listening to his incredible road trip playlist that's the perfect mix of 90s and early 2000s alternative and rock featuring both mainstream and indie artists, and playing fifty questions. It started as twenty questions, but we lost track and kept going until we got to our hotel in Pacific Grove. We practice our air guitar, drum solos, and horrible singing in the best hour-long car karaoke on the final stretch of the drive. Once we park, he cups the back of my head and leans in to kiss me again. "Hope you don't mind the hotel I chose. There was nothing available in Carmel and this is close, plus it has a great view of the water."

"It's perfect. I would have been happy with sleeping bags and a tent. I didn't expect you to get a hotel."

"Figured this time of year we could get rain and after a day in the water, I want a hot shower and an actual bed. Let's get checked in and we can decide what we want to do tonight. It will be an early morning for us, but it's not so late we can't find something to do tonight."

"I know the perfect place. Low-key restaurant and bar with patio seating. They usually have live music on Saturday nights."

"Perfect."

I'm tempted to tell him to cancel the second room, but something tells me he wouldn't go for that idea. He comes around to my side to open the door for me, but I'm already out and closing the door. We walk hand-in-hand into the lobby to check in. When we get to the front counter, I overhear the woman next to me talking to one of the staff members. "I don't know how this could happen. I have the confirmation right here. One room. Two beds. And I pre-paid. Now you're telling me you don't have a record of the reservation. But money already came out of my account. What am I supposed to do?"

"I'm so sorry. We're trying to find you a room with another facility. We are at capacity tonight."

Jameson looks down at me and his eyes shift toward the woman and her three kids who are getting antsy sitting in the lobby. I nod, answering his silent question. He gets the staff member's attention. "Excuse me. We have two rooms, but the friends traveling with us ended up not coming. We can give this family our second room. I made non-refundable reservations, but I'm sure, given the circumstances, we can figure out something."

"Absolutely," the older gentleman says as he walks around the counter. "If I can get your ID, I can pull up your reservation and move things around."

Jameson hands him his ID and shows him the electronic reservation.

"Okay, Mr. Jameson, you have two rooms. One king and one with two double beds. Do you have a preference for which to keep?"

"No, but I think they likely need the two beds."

We take our key cards and head back to the Expedition to get our stuff. Once we have everything in our room, I unpack my bag. I'm not one of those people who can live out of a suitcase, even for just a night or two. Apparently, Jameson is the same way because he also unpacks after putting our dive gear against the wall.

When he's done unpacking, he sits on the end of the bed. I turn to face him. The only thing I've thought about since our first kiss is kissing him again. The brief moment in the hotel parking lot was a tease. I need more. I stalk across the small space between the dresser and bed and step between his legs. His arm circles around my waist. My fingers thread through his hair as I slowly lower to sit on his thigh. His thumb caresses my cheek as he leans in to kiss me. Without breaking the kiss, I rotate slightly and press my chest against his. He slows us and pulls back. "Just kissing tonight, sunshine."

I grumble my protest. "I don't think I can sleep next to you and not do more than kiss."

He lifts me off his lap and sets me on the corner of the bed. Then he quickly pulls down the covers and rearranges the pillows. Including using the long decorative bolster pillow as a divider. "Pick whatever side you want. You stay on your half. I'll stay on mine."

You have got to be kidding me! Proof my life isn't a romance novel. Because if it were, as soon as we realized there was only one bed, we'd have to bang. Instead, there's going to be a pile of pillows between us.

Chapter 12

We find parking in the large public lot in the center of town, which is convenient. Sadie takes my hand and leads me down the street. "Two of my favorite bars are this way. I think we should start at the one that's technically a restaurant or pub because they close at 11. Then we can walk a few blocks to the bar. They're open until two. I don't think either one of us plans to be out that late since we're diving in the morning, but it will be nice to have the option."

"Sounds perfect."

We get to the pub on the corner and there's a crowd enjoying live music on the outdoor patio. As we make our way to the bar inside, I find myself counting exits and plotting escapes. Once a Marine, always a Marine. I can't stop myself from doing this and I don't bother trying to anymore. When we get to the front of the line, I stand directly behind Sadie, blocking the view of her ass from the two guys sitting at the end of the bar who haven't taken their eyes off her since she walked into the room. My hand rests on the small of her back as I silently tell them with my action that she's taken. Sadie orders a stout, then tosses her hair over her shoulder. "What do you want?"

"Club soda with lime." I set cash on the bar to cover both our drinks.

"You can have one drink. We'll be out for hours."

I shake my head. "Nope. If I'm driving, I'm in control. I never drink if I'm getting behind the wheel and usually not when someone else is either. Just in case. I have one or two at home, but that's it."

She reaches for my hand on her back and guides it around her side to rest on her waist while we wait for our drinks. My fingers instantly dig into her skin as I press my body against hers. My free hand brushes her hair off her neck. When my movements stop, she bats her long eyelashes at me. "Do it. You know you want to."

My lips press against her neck. *Screwed. I'm completely screwed.*

I knew it when we kissed in traffic this afternoon, but I tried to deny it. Now that I'm kissing her in public, digging my fingers into her skin, and silently claiming her, I know that she's everything I want.

Once we have our drinks, we make our way to the patio. We find one available seat on the bench against the fence, so I take it, and then guide her onto my lap. "Comfy, sunshine?"

She nods as her face closes in on mine. Her forehead rests against my temple. "I could get used to this."

"Me too," I admit. "Everything feels easy when we're together."

"Agreed. That's why I think we need to give this a chance. Not just while on the trip, but when we get home. No pressure. Remember what I told you the other day? I'm not looking for wedding vows and baby strollers."

She might not want those things now, but she could in the future, and I've never felt the pull toward either of those things. It doesn't feel fair to enter into a relationship when you're unsure what you want in the future. That's one reason I haven't committed to anything long-term before. The other is I didn't want to leave someone behind if I didn't make it home. Now that combat isn't an excuse, the only one that remains is not knowing how I want my future to look.

While I'm lost in my thoughts, Sadie's singing along with the music. When her beer is empty, she stands and takes my hands in hers, pulling me to my feet so we can dance. I don't dance. Ever. But once I'm on my feet, my body sways with the music, and my arms hook around her waist. We dance through the next four songs. She sits on my thigh for the last two songs of the set and quietly sings along.

After dropping our empty glasses onto the cart by the gate, we make our way down the street to the bar. Sadie squeals with excitement when she reads the chalkboard on the wall by the door. "It's karaoke night. This is going to be fun. I know the perfect song."

"Well, you warmed up while singing along with the last two songs. I can't wait to hear what you choose."

She gives me a mischievous smirk. "Not for me. You." Then she darts through the crowd to the DJ table where she fills out a slip.

When she gets back to me, I'm standing at one of the tall tables for two. "That better be for you, sunshine."

"Not just me."

Ten minutes later, the DJ calls out, "Next up, the Care Bear duo. Sunshine and Grumpy Bear, make your way to the stage."

The crowd laughs at our names. Applause fills the room as Sadie drags me to the stage. She hands me a hot pink rhinestone microphone while keeping the non-bejeweled solid black option for herself. "Really, sunshine? I think hot pink is your color, not mine."

"You'll understand once the song starts."

My lips press against her ears. "What did you do?"

She doesn't have time to reply and I understand why I'm the one holding the rhinestone microphone when *Don't Go Breaking My Heart* starts. I stumble through Elton John's parts while keeping my eyes fixed on the screen. Sadie belts out Kiki Dee's without needing the lyrics. When I lose my place, Sadie takes over both parts and finishes the song for us. We leave the stage in a fit of laughter. When we return to our table, she stands in front of me, loops her arms over my shoulders, and stares into my eyes. "What did you think?"

"It was a lot more fun than I expected."

Once she raises onto her tiptoes, I know what she's hinting at, so I capture her lips with mine. We are that ridiculous couple that needs to get a room. When we finally part, I take her hand in mine and lead her out of the bar and to the parking lot.

Sleeping next to her and keeping my hands to myself is no longer my plan. I want the brunette beauty wrapped in my arms tonight. When we get to our room, I kick off my shoes and pull my shirt over my head before opening the dresser drawer to grab the pajama bottoms and shirt I packed.

Sadie sighs as she looks in her open drawer. "I forgot pajamas. How did I manage that? I guess I'm sleeping in my tank top."

I place my gray shirt over her shoulder as I walk toward the bathroom. "Here. You can wear this. It will be long on you, like a nightshirt."

After changing into sleep pants and brushing my teeth, I return to the bedroom area and find her wearing my shirt. While she brushes her teeth, I untuck the sheets and blankets and crawl into bed. I leave the decorative pillow pile between us, not because I want it, but in case she does.

As she slides into bed, she throws the pillows onto the floor and scoots to the center. She places her head on my chest before pulling the covers up over both of us. "You didn't think I was going to agree to that ridiculous pile of pillows, did you?"

I reach for the bedside lamp and turn it off. "Maybe when I first set it up. But I almost tossed them aside when you were in the bathroom."

"Goodnight, grumpy bear."

"Night, sunshine."

Ten minutes later, she's asleep. I expect to spend the next hour staring at the ceiling. Instead, sleep overtakes me less than fifteen minutes later and for the first time in longer than I can remember, I sleep for a solid six hours.

Chapter 13

When I wake in the morning, Jameson's already awake. His thumb strokes my cheek. "Hey, sunshine. You ready for our adventure?"

I quickly kiss him, then hop out of bed to get ready. "Looking forward to showing you my favorite dive spot. Then maybe we can enjoy some time at the beach."

He sits on the edge of the bed and reaches his arm out to me. I accept it and sit on his thigh. He kisses me softly while his thumb caresses my cheek. "That was my thought, too. I already packed our food and drinks in the smaller cooler. I made dinner reservations for us here in Pacific Grove. We have a table for two next to a fireplace at six. We'll have time to shower and change before dinner."

"Sounds fancy."

"I was going for romantic, but I'll take fancy."

My arms loop over his shoulders. "It's definitely romantic. Thanks for planning it. I was thinking of pizza at my favorite place."

His hand cups my cheek and he stares into my eyes. "I'm not one to pass up a great pizza, but I want something special tonight. Now, let's go to your favorite dive spot. I can't wait to see it."

After a few hours exploring the water and capturing some incredible photos with my underwater camera, we store our gear in the back of the Expedition and head to the beach to enjoy the rest of our afternoon. Jameson is full of surprises. He not only brought a large beach blanket and towels, but he also has a pop-up shade canopy and two beach games—corn hole and disc golf.

Once the blanket and cooler are under the canopy, Jameson guides me onto his lap and coats me with sunblock. He spends extra time massaging my shoulders and lower back. It has nothing to do with protecting my skin from the sun and everything to do with enjoying touching me. I noticed he always kept me within reach during our dive. I lean against him and enjoy the feel of his arms tightening around me. He kisses the top of my head. "I see why you love it here. The dive was incredible. The beach is gorgeous. This could easily become my favorite spot."

"I don't mind sharing it with you," I rotate slightly, so we're facing each other. "It won't cost you much."

"You can have anything you want, sunshine."

"Just promise you'll never bring another girl here. Let this be a place that's ours."

His hand rests on my cheek. "That's a simple request to honor because I don't want anyone else. Only you." He guides my face toward him and kisses me.

We spend the next half hour kissing. Then we show off our competitive sides by playing disc golf and corn hole. He kicks my ass at both but tries not to rub it in too much.

Chapter 14

After our incredible dinner, I take Sadie for an evening stroll by the beach before heading back to our hotel room. As soon as I lock the hotel door, I can't resist kissing her. I pin her to the wall with my body and box her in with my arms against the wall. "Sadie, tell me this isn't a good idea. Tell me it's too soon."

But she doesn't. She shakes her head as she loops her arms over my shoulder. "Kiss me."

My mouth claims hers, and my tongue slips between her lips. I'm not sure how long I have her pinned against the wall, but soon, I guide her to the bed. I sit and pull her onto my lap. Her knees dig into the mattress on each side of my hips as she rocks against me. The right thing to do is stop kissing her, stand up, and get out of the hotel room. If we sit on this bed much longer, I'm going to throw her onto the center of it, strip her out of her clothes, and spend the rest of the night seeing how many orgasms I can give her. My brain knows we should stop, but my heart is screaming '*Mine, mine, mine.*' Or maybe it's my dick. All I know is I never want to kiss anyone else again. I need her the way I need air, the way the ocean needs the moon, and the way plants need the sun—for survival. She has awakened something in me from the moment I saw her. She brought me back to life.

Her nails scrape down my neck, then across my shoulders. Her hands caress down my sides until she gets to the hem of my shirt. She glides it up my body. I break our kiss just long enough to raise my arms over my head and let her drag the shirt off me before she yanks hers off, revealing a gray bra with lace details. "We should stop," I whisper against her neck before peppering her collarbone with kisses.

"No," she commands as she reaches for my belt. She sucks my earlobe between her lips. "Griffin Henry Jameson, stop overthinking and just go with it."

My name sounds like the most beautiful song performed. "How'd you figure it out?"

"I looked at your ID when you gave it to the clerk." Her lips cover mine as she unbuttons and unzips my jeans.

My hands cup her breasts. They're the perfect handful. I suck in a breath when she gasps and moans as she rocks against my erection. "Naked, Griff. We need to be naked."

I gently toss her onto the center of the bed, slide out of my jeans, and pull her pants off as I kick my shoes off.

I'm suddenly very thankful for only packing my Vans for the trip. I don't have to deal with socks. She's a vision of beauty spread out on the center of the bed with her chestnut hair fanned across the pillows. "Are you sure about this, sunshine?"

"Yes. I want you. I'm on the pill and I packed condoms. They're in the top dresser drawer. Use one."

I grab a handful and throw them onto the nightstand. Then I crawl onto the bed next to her. I prop onto my left side. My fingers trail up her thigh. "You're beautiful."

"The view from here's not so bad either." She reaches her right hand out, cups my cheek, and guides my face to hers. "Kiss me," she requests on shallow breath.

As our tongues tangle, my fingers trace the bouquet of wildflowers that covers her hip and thigh. I can't wait to examine her beautiful tattoos closer later. I'm curious if the vine of ivy down her side leads to anything on her back. But my tattoo exploration is going to have to wait. I have more important things on my mind right now.

She rotates slightly, so she's also on her side and scoots closer to me before placing her leg on mine. It's like she's calling my dick home, where it longs to be. I'm torn between wanting to savor every moment, taking in everything, and longing to be inside her, holding her down, and fucking her hard before flipping her over and taking her from behind. As if she can read my mind, she trails her hand down my chest. "Stop overthinking. It's not like you only get one chance. We can do it all. I like it all. Do whatever you want with me, Griff. I'm yours."

Mine. She's mine. I know as soon as we do this, I won't want to give her up. My brain tells me this is a bad idea.

We're moving too fast, but the rest of me doesn't care. I want her.

No, scratch that. I need her.

I lower my face to her neck and slowly lick down her chest while rotating us so she's on her back and I'm over her. I suck one nipple into my mouth, swirl my tongue around it, then pull back, gently biting before I do the same with the other. She widens her legs and wraps them around my hips, locking her ankles against my back. Her hand reaches between her thighs and she begins fingering herself. I push her hand away, replace her fingers with mine, and growl, "Mine."

My lips trail down her stomach. While one hand rotates between massaging each breast, the other digs into her hip, testing how much pressure she can take.

Her hand covers mine, applying more pressure to her breast. "I like it rough, Griff. Please don't be gentle. I want bruises shaped like your fingertips and scratches. I want your mark all over me."

If my girl wants it rough, that's what she's going to get. My hands clasp against her hips and I flip her over. "Get your beautiful ass up and support yourself on your arms, sunshine." I knee her thighs apart, then smack her ass as I take in the gorgeous tattoo covering her back. The ivy vines on her left side wrap around to a field of flowers that covers her shoulder blade. The other side of her back is a stack of books. Once she's how I want her, I trail my finger down her spine and watch goosebumps form. I immediately repeat the action with my tongue. "I'm spending all night inside you. I'm going to fuck you from behind until you're exhausted, then I'm going to flip you over, put your ankles on my shoulders, and make you come until you beg me to stop because you can't handle another orgasm."

She turns her head to look at me over her shoulder. "I won't tell you to stop. I meant what I said. You can do whatever you want with me."

Whatever self-control I'm trying to grasp disappears. I reach for the stack of condoms, tear one open, and slide it on. "Limits?"

"None that are in play right now. I don't share. No one watches. That sort of thing. No videos. No pictures."

There's no way I'm sharing her, so those limits aren't an issue. "Safe word?"

"Taco."

As she says the word, I notice the hair tie on her wrist. I remove it, gather her long locks into my hands, and secure it with the simple white elastic band. Then I wrap her hair around my wrist and hand. I tug gently, gauging her reaction. Then a second and third time. Each a little harder. The third time gets the reaction I'm waiting for. She whimpers with surprise, but not pain. I want control, but don't want to hurt her. My fingers press into her warm cunt. "Ready for me, sunshine?"

"Yes," she whimpers as she presses her ass against me. "Give me that dick, big guy. I need it." Hearing her beg for me is incredible. Maybe she needs me the way I need her. I stroke my dick three times before sliding into her. Each inch I press into her has her asking for more. "Not so slow. I want it all."

I use her hair to guide her off her arms until her back is against my chest and I'm buried balls deep. I release her ponytail and wrap that arm around her waist, holding her against me as I rock in and out of her. My other hand presses against her neck, applying light pressure. I want to ease her into this because I'm not sure if she's experienced with it or how much she's comfortable with. She places one hand on mine, encouraging me. Then she whispers, "More," so I press a little harder.

My lips press against her ear. "That's it, sunshine. Take this dick. You take it so well."

Her free hand squeezes my thigh as she rocks against me. My hand on her waist slides down her stomach until my thumb reaches her clit. I gently flick it, then pull out of her until just the tip remains. My hand lessens the pressure on her neck.

"Nooo," she whines as she presses her ass against me, trying to get more of me, but I hold her in place.

"Tell me what you want, sunshine."

"More."

"Beg for it."

"Give me that good dick, please."

I adjust slightly so my hands are each cupping one breast. I massage each while twisting the nipples until she cries out in a combination of pleasure and pain from the pinching. Then I slam into her. My hands release her breast. One massages her ass while the other presses her forward until she's supporting herself on her forearms. My hands dig into her hips as I rock against her, sliding in and out, riding her until we're both covered in a thin layer of sweat. Each whimper, murmur, and mewl sends a spark through me. I love knowing I'm the one bringing her so much pleasure. My thumb teases her clit and I feel her walls tighten, so I pause my movement. "Nooo, I was so close."

My hand smacks against her ass. "You can't come until I tell you to. Beg for it, sunshine."

"I need it. I need your dick inside me. I need the weight of your body against me. Fuck me until I can't see straight, Griff."

With a request like that, there's no holding back any longer. I gather her ponytail around my hand again because I know from her reaction earlier that she likes having her hair pulled. Then I slam into her. I work in and out of her until just before we come. Then I use her ponytail to guide her back into my arms. Once she's against me, I whisper in her ear. "Come. Strangle my cock and milk it for everything I have."

Just as she tightens around me, my hand presses against her neck. We both come hard and then I collapse onto the bed, bringing her down with me until she's plastered against me. My lips press against her forehead as I gently massage her throat. "That was incredible."

"You have ruined me for anyone else. It's never been like that before. No one has ever just known what I like or want without me giving them very specific instructions and even then, it's not quite what I want."

My brain, dick, and heart like hearing that. She's mine. I grab tissues from the nightstand to take care of the condom because I don't want to move us yet. When she realizes what I'm doing, she takes the tissues from my hand, uses them to slide the condom off, and wraps it. Then she stretches across me to drop the bundle in the trash can. Her gorgeous tits are within reach, so I massage them, then kiss each one. "I want to fuck these next."

"Without a condom. Then you can paint me with your cum before washing it off in the shower."

I'm usually good for two or three orgasms a night, but I need a little time between rounds. Not tonight. My dick springs to attention with that offer. She breaks into an adorable giggle and the freckles on her cheeks are more noticeable when she smiles. "Someone likes that offer."

My hands cup her cheeks and I kiss her. "Get comfy, sunshine. We're just getting started."

Chapter 15

After Griff paints me with his cum, he carries me to the shower. I don't have to look in the mirror to know he wrote 'MINE' down my torso. I felt the shape of the letters and watched the goofy grin on his face when he did it. I'm an independent woman who has never relied on a man. I shouldn't like it, but I can't help it. I love it. The grumpy former Marine who is in search of direction somehow found me. And everything about us feels right. I know we're still getting to know each other, but something tells me he's the one I've been hoping to find one day. The one who accepts everything about me, has common interests, and can be more than a good time in the sack.

His lips haven't left mine, even when turning on the water. Once it's warm, he steps into the small stall and pulls the door shut behind us, while keeping me secure in his other arm. He somehow manages to wash both of us without setting me down. My legs wrapped around his hips, helps free my hands to wash his hair while he scrubs shampoo and condition through mine. "Close your eyes and tip your head back, I'm going to rinse your hair."

Once we are completely rinsed, he turns off the water and steps out of the shower. When he sets me on my feet outside the shower stall, he wraps his arms around me, and I let myself melt into his embrace. His lips glide down the side of my neck. "I wasn't too rough, right?"

"Not at all."

He wraps a towel around me, then quickly dries himself before tying his towel around his waist. Then he takes my comb from my hands and begins gently working it through the tangles. He places his palm in front of me. "Give me the leave-in conditioner or whatever you use. Let me take care of these tangles for you."

"You don't have to. I can do it."

His other hand gently smacks my ass. "Hush. Don't argue. It's called aftercare. Let me take care of you."

This is unexpected in the best way. Aftercare is usually only a shower and maybe sleeping next to someone, in hopes of another round later. Once he's done combing the conditioner through my curls, he sections my hair into two parts and surprises me when he braids them into two perfect Dutch braids. "Wow! This is impressive."

My stomach rumbles lightly, and I hope he doesn't notice. I'm hungry after our marathon sex session. He doesn't react to the quiet growl, so I'm certain he didn't hear it.

His warm lips press against my cheek. "Oldest of four. Two sisters and a brother. Mom and Dad were both out the door before we woke in the morning. I got the girls ready for school and my brother made breakfast and packed lunches."

This is the first time he has said anything about his family outside of ordering the birthday gifts. It's nice he's opening up to me. My eyes lock on his through the mirror reflection. "Do you miss them?"

"Yeah. But I talk to everyone at least once a week and there's a massive family text chat. I don't feel like I miss anything. We've been apart for half my life, so it's our normal."

I want to know more about them, but something tells me not to push too quickly. He'll tell me on his terms. We finish getting ready for bed and head to the bedroom area. I grab his shirt from the dresser drawer where I stashed it this morning. The cotton materials feel soft against my skin and smells like him. I have never been the type to steal someone's shirt, but this one is definitely coming home with me unless he takes it when we pack.

While I pull his shirt on, he gathers snacks from the mini fridge and our coolers. We climb into bed, and he guides me into his arms. "You look cute in my T-shirt."

"Thanks for letting me steal it. I'm not sure how I forgot pajamas."

"I still think it's funny you remembered condoms, but not something to sleep in." He hands me a flavored water. Then he opens the cake box. He tugs on the shirt's hem. "I've decided pajamas are overrated and naked would be better."

I chug half the water before I respond. "If I was naked right now, neither of us would get any sleep tonight."

He stabs his fork into the cake and holds it out to me. "True. Very true. I'm going to feed you cake, then we're going to sleep. My alarm is already set. Do you want anything besides cake? We still have a sandwich and anything else you packed."

I scoot closer to him so I can rest against his chest. "This is perfect."

Chapter 16

Sadie has been asleep for almost five hours. I fell asleep after our shower, but then the insomnia took over an hour later. I pace across the floor from the hotel door to the window and back. I toss the camo bouncy ball from one hand to the other. If bouncing it against the wall, door, or ceiling wouldn't risk waking her, I'd do that, but the last thing I want is for her to see me like this. She doesn't need to know that I lose myself to thoughts so dark I can't shut them off. When she shifts in her sleep and reaches her arm out, I know she's looking for me. I stop walking and hope she settles. But she doesn't. Instead, she sits up. She stretches her arms over her head before wiping the sleep from her eyes. "Hey, why aren't you in bed?"

"Couldn't sleep." It's not a lie. At least not completely.

Her eyes dart from mine to my hands, where I'm clutching the bouncy ball tightly. So tightly my nails are digging into my palm. She touches my side of the bed. It's likely cold because I've been out of bed for hours. "How long have you been up?"

"Almost four hours," I admit as my eyes drop to my feet.

"Nightmare?"

"No." When I don't offer anything else, I expect her to give up. But she doesn't.

"Is it just insomnia or something else?"

Why is it so hard to be normal? Why can't I just tell her?

She crawls across the bed to me, raises to her knees, then kisses the center of my chest. "I'm not going to push, but I'm here when you want to tell me." Her arms loop over my shoulders and she pulls me toward her. "Promise not to push me away."

I wish it was that easy. That I could simply promise not to. But it doesn't work that way. I don't plan to push her away and it's the last thing I want to do, but there's no guarantee it won't happen. "I don't plan to do it. I'll try not to. That's the best I can give."

Her lips press against mine. "Okay. That's a start. Come back to bed. Even if you can't sleep. Just rest with me. We can watch a movie or something if that will help."

I crawl into bed, wrap my arms around her, and haul her onto my chest. I need every part of her touching me.

Halfway home, our conversation goes quiet. Not because Sadie stops talking or asking questions, but because I close up. I stop engaging. She gets one-word responses, nods, and grunts. After days of not keeping my hands off her, they're gripping the steering wheel so tightly my knuckles are white, and my palms have indentations from my nails.

Countless reasons for why I'm not good enough for her and why being with her is wrong race through my mind. None of it has anything to do with her brother's misogynistic belief in the 'bro code,' and everything to do with my fear that my insomnia and nightmares will get worse again. At their worst, they led me to scream in my sleep and I've woken to holes in my walls I don't remember punching. Being with me has the potential to hurt her. I can't risk that. I would never forgive myself if I didn't protect her the way I didn't protect my training partner the day our careers ended.

I know all the dark thoughts running through my mind are bullshit and I need to call my shrink, go to some group sessions, and talk about everything. That always helps. But instead of telling Sadie the truth about what I'm thinking and feeling, I shut down. When I told Sadie I would try not to push her away, I meant it. I didn't intend to, but it happened and once my brain went down that path, I couldn't stop myself. The shittiest part is when I pull into her driveway and unpack her things from my Expedition, I know I'm not only going to push her away. I'm going to go dark and avoid her completely.

I drop her bags in her entryway. She steps forward and loops her arms over my neck. "I don't know what's going on. I didn't push on the drive." Her lips press against my cheek. "Let's order dinner and relax. Or we can skip dinner and head to bed. You'll feel better if you sleep. Stay? Please."

My fingers graze through her hair before I step back. "It's going to be another night of little to no sleep. I'll feel more comfortable if I'm not keeping you up."

She leans in for a kiss and as much as I want to take my time with it, I keep it short. As soon as I break our physical connection, I shut the door. "Lock up, sunshine."

Then I drive to Devin's, unload my stuff into the garage, and immediately head into my room.

Chapter 17

As I lock the door, I'm stunned by how quickly he walked away. "What just happened?" I mumble, before grabbing my dive gear and carrying it to my room.

Olivia's footsteps on the stairs startle me. Since she doesn't have a car, I don't always know when she's home. "Hey, how was your trip? I scooted upstairs when I saw Jameson's Expedition because I figured he'd be staying for a bit and wanted to give you privacy."

"The trip was wonderful. The drive back was weird."

She grabs my overnight bag and backpack. Then follows me to my room. "What happened?"

I put my gear in my closet. I'll deal with it tomorrow. Then I collapse, snow angel style, on my full-size bed.

"I don't know. Things were great. We had so much fun. Our conversation felt natural. There were no awkward pauses. The physical connection was there. I thought he got over whatever was holding him back from giving us a chance. But everything changed in an instant. His answers to questions or responses to my comments became single words or grunts. I don't know what happened."

The bed depresses next to me. "There was no sign that something was bothering him?"

I would never share about Griff's nightmares or how he paced the hotel room. That isn't my story to share. I shift slightly and look up at her. "Everything was perfect. Better than I expected. I don't know what happened." My voice breaks when I try to share more. Instead of talking, I roll onto my side and cry.

Her fingers comb through my hair. "It's okay. Let it out. You'll feel better."

Olivia is the second oldest of six. She instantly shifts to big sister mode. She sits with me and listens to me cry for the next hour. Then she pulls the covers down on my bed and tells me to rest. A half hour later, she brings in chips, salsa, and queso dip. "There's ice cream in the freezer for later. You, me, a movie binge, and snacks. No talking about that grumpy man unless you want to."

She turns on the TV, logs into our household movie streaming account, and selects one of our shared favorites. *Girls Just Wanna Have Fun* always makes us laugh and brings us out of a funk. I think we watched it for two days straight the weekend her divorce was official. Olivia is the kindest person I've ever known. Her ex-husband was a dumbass for walking away from her

There aren't many people in this world who are genuine without wanting anything in return.

When the movie is over, she collects our food and trash. "Ready for ice cream?"

I nod. "Thank you, Livs."

"You're welcome. We'll get through this together, okay? No matter if it's a simple misunderstanding or something else. I'm here."

I really hope it's only a misunderstanding. But the knot in my gut tells me it's something more, and it's not anything I can change. It's all on Griffin Henry Jameson, the most frustrating man I've ever known.

After two days without hearing from Griff, I know whatever spell we were under on the coast is broken. He doesn't want me and he's too much of a chicken shit to tell me. My phone calls go straight to voicemail. My text messages aren't read. I rescheduled my appointments and got someone to cover my shifts at the theater. I haven't left my bedroom since Olivia tucked me in and tried to mend my heart with snacks and ice cream.

My phone vibrates on my nightstand. My heart leaps, hoping it's him. Then it sinks to my stomach when it's not. I've never been the person who spends days in bed crying over someone while wearing their shirt. But here I am—a breakup cliché.

> Sorry it took so long to respond. I was on a work trip and so was Stefan. Our schedules are total opposites right now. I had to confirm with him before giving you this info. Yes, he would love to talk to Jameson. Quote 'He sounds perfect for a secured communications position with us. I need his information ASAP. Tell Sadie to have him call me. Any time, day or night. I need to talk to him before another agency finds him.' I'm attaching Stefan's contact info.

> Thank you. I appreciate it.

I write down the information on a sticky note. I keep a stack of them on my nightstand for those middle of the night thoughts I don't want to forget. Since Griff isn't looking at my texts, I have to rely on the old-fashioned way of communicating with a boy who doesn't give two shits about you—passing a note through your friend or sibling.

Devin told me he was stopping by this afternoon because he was worried about me since I hadn't been by the restaurant. I'm almost positive it's a ploy to find out what happened on the dive trip.

When my bedroom door creaks open without a knock, I know it's Devin. I roll over, then sit up. "Hi," I say sleepily.

"Girl, what is going on? You look like death warmed over and you're never asleep at 3pm."

"Nothing. I'm just tired. I took a few days off and decided to treat myself to a staycation."

Devin plops onto the bed and stretches his legs out while resting his back against the headboard. "You've always been a horrible liar. It's a good thing you never learned to play poker because the little creases that form on your forehead when you lie are an easy tell. I want the truth, Sadie. Did something happen between you and Jameson?"

I rest my head on my big brother's shoulder. "Don't go thinking he took advantage of me. Anything that happened was mutual, other than when he just stopped talking to me."

"When did that happen?"

"On the drive home. Then he barely kissed me at the door, pulled it shut, and told me to lock up. He hasn't answered my calls or even read my texts since."

"His phone is off. I can't reach him on it either. Unless I see him at work or home, he's not talking to me. And he's barely saying a word to anyone."

I grab the sticky note and hold it out to him. "Can you give him this? A friend's husband is ex-military and wants to talk to him about a secured communications job."

Devin glances at it before shoving it back into my hand. "Nope. Giggles, this is one you're going to have to handle. Take it to him yourself. He's at the restaurant and will be there until closing. You two are adults and can figure this out. You owe it to yourself, Sadie. Force him to talk to you. Or say whatever you want so you can move forward without wondering what happened."

I huff. "Just do it, please."

"Nope. Get out of bed. Change clothes. Go yell at him. Then head up to the canyon, stare at the sky, and clear your head. You always feel better after that. Let me know when you get home, so I don't worry about you."

He kisses the top of my head and then slides off the bed. "I mean it, Sadie. Get this taken care of with him. Then move on. You deserve someone who puts your feelings first and makes you a priority. If he can't be that person, fuck him."

I wipe the tears from my eyes with the shirt's collar. And silently reprimand myself for inhaling, hoping the shirt still smells like Griff's cologne. "That's the problem, Devin. I already did."

He grabs the small stuffed teddy bear I keep on my dresser and chucks it at me. "Gross. I didn't need to know. I assumed, but I didn't need confirmation."

After Devin leaves, I change clothes for the first time in days. When I get to the front door, I turn and look at the stairs. Olivia is home and she would come with me if I ask. But, deep down, I know I need to do this by myself. I grab my keys off the hook by the door and head toward the restaurant.

Chapter 18

I have spent the last three days working my shifts at the restaurant, working out, and riding my bike on the trails. I kept my phone turned off. I know that means text messages show as unread. I don't want to leave her on read and not respond, so I chose the chicken shit way out of this mess and hid. I barely spoke to anyone at work. Thankfully, I'm only working shifts in the kitchen, so I don't have to be friendly behind the bar. Earlier tonight, before he left, Devin asked me what was wrong, and I told him some bullshit half-truth about being in a funk and that I was working on it. I *am* in a funk, but I'm not working through it. I'm avoiding it.

It's Friday night, just before midnight. I'm plating fries into a sliders basket and I'm in the shittiest mood I've been in since three months after my injury. Each day since leaving Sadie's house, I've become grumpier and shut down more. Hunter and Luke aren't even talking to me tonight unless it's about a ticket because I've snapped at them multiple times.

The back door to the kitchen flies open. Sadie storms over to me. "Good, you're not dead or something. You're simply a jackass. I really thought you were different. I was so dumb to fall for the lines about giving us a chance and wanting this to be more." Her palm smacks against my cheek. I deserve it. I deserve more, really. "The shittiest part is you didn't have to put on an act. We could have had a few nights of fun and walked away. You didn't have to lie to me. You didn't have to feed me lines."

She reaches into the back pocket of her skin-tight jeans and pulls out a folded piece of paper. She slams it against the prep station. "Here. Even though I mean nothing to you. You're still important to me. I contacted a friend's husband. He's ex-military and works for a private company. They need someone with your language skills and communications background. They'd love to talk to you. I already told Stefan about you. I just left out the part about you being a lying piece of shit." She turns and takes two steps to the door, but then stops and looks back. "In case it's not clear, I'm done. Taco!"

Before I can respond, she runs out the door.

Luke and Hunter are both silent. I turn toward them. "Get back to work," I snap. Then I shove the paper from

Sadie into my apron pocket. I don't have time to deal with any of this right now.

Thirty minutes later, the door to the kitchen opens and my best friend storms in. "What the fuck did you do to her?"

Luke pushes me away from the grill. "Get out. Hunter and I have this. Go deal with whatever's going on. I keep my mouth shut about a lot around here. I haven't said a word about your grumpy disposition when you started here or how you've been a total jackass this week. I figured you were going through something. But if she so much as gave you the time of day, you're a lucky bastard because Sadie's incredible. Fix it or if you can't fix it, you at the very least owe her an apology."

I throw my hands up in frustration. "I know. I royally fucked up. I don't know why and I damn sure don't know how to fix it."

Devin steps toward me. "It's taking all my restraint not to beat the shit out of you right now. Turn on your fucking phone. Read her messages and respond. Or better yet, go talk to her. Get on your knees and beg her to forgive you. It's really not that fucking hard. *Talk. To. Her.* Tell her whatever's going through your head. All that shit you push deep down inside and ignore, open your mouth, and say the words. You don't get to act like you want to be friends with someone and then push them away. I'm sure something else happened between you two for her to be this upset, but she's not telling me."

I kick the wall out of frustration with myself. "Is she at her house?"

"No. She sent me a text and told me she needed to clear her head and she was going to photograph the sky. I'm assuming it's the spot she always goes to in the canyon. I can tell you where."

I grab my jacket and keys. "I know where it is. We ran into each other during the meteor shower."

When I get to the top of the trail, I expect to find her with her camera gear set up. Instead, she's sitting on the bench, with her arms wrapped around her knees and her face pressed against her legs. I already know I'm an asshole, but hearing her cry drives it home.

She jumps when I sit next to her. I don't sit at the opposite end of the bench from her. I sit right next to her and wrap my arm around her. "I'm sorry. I know those two words don't change anything. They don't take away the fact I was a total dick and disappeared for days. They won't mean anything without a behavior change. Can I tell you why I did it?"

She leans against me and wraps her arms around my waist. "I should tell you to fuck off. But for some reason, I can't. I think it's because I love you. And that's the shittiest part about this situation. I fell in love with you. And you threw me away."

My heart sinks into my stomach. "I didn't mean to make you feel like I threw you away. What I'm about to tell you is probably going to sound like bullshit excuses, but it's all true and it's something I've never shared with anyone except my shrink. Let me say it all and then you can tell me to fuck off or that you're willing to let me grovel and make it up to you. Devin told me I needed to get on my knees and beg for your forgiveness."

She chuckles against my chest. "If I decide to forgive you, you can get on your knees, but it will be for something besides begging."

I know I shouldn't, but I can't stop myself. I twist her ponytail around my hand and gently tug. "Behave."

"Make me."

I tug again, this time enough so her head rises from my chest. I stare into her caramel eyes. "I really hope you forgive me because I don't want to learn to live without my sunshine."

Her fingertips trail up my chest, then trace my jaw. "Tell me whatever you want to tell me. However much you can. I don't need every detail tonight, but I need to know why you disappeared and if there's anything I could have done differently, or if there's anything you need from me, if this happens again."

The words pour out of me easier than they ever have before, "I've seen a lot of really dark shit that I don't talk about, and I'll likely never share. Sometimes the memories of those things creep in and I can't push them away. About a year before my injury, we lost two members of our team. I know it's not my fault. I know there was nothing I could have done to stop it or to change the outcome. I wasn't even there. The darkest thing that takes over is that it should have been me." Without realizing I'm doing it, I haul her onto my lap and nuzzle my face against her neck. I need her close.

"Oh, Griff. If you weren't there, of course, it's not your fault. You don't have to tell me the details, but I see from your reaction it must have been horrible. I can't imagine what it was like for your team. Survivor's guilt is real. You need to talk to someone."

"I do. But sometimes it's not enough. Then nights like the one in the hotel happen. After so much good in my life, the darkness tells me I don't deserve it and that if I get too close, I'll lose you. That I don't deserve you. That I won't be able to protect you. The way I didn't protect myself or my partner during the training that injured both of us." I know the training injury was out of my control. I wasn't in charge. I had nothing to do with any of it. Someone else made the mistakes, and we paid the price. But knowing it doesn't mean the dark thoughts don't come and when they do, it's so easy to believe them.

She kisses one cheek, then the other, before rubbing the tip of her nose against mine. "I'm right here, Griff. I'm safe. The only way you'll lose me is if you push me away or you run. You did both of those things. You let the darkness win. Don't do it again."

"I'll try my best not to and if I think I'm going to, I'll talk to you," I pause for a moment and then tell her the one thing I haven't admitted to anyone. "I started seeing my shrink for regular appointments again and I'm going to attend a group session with other vets."

"There's nothing wrong with therapy. It's not anything to be ashamed of. I think it's important to have people to talk to." She kisses the tip of my nose. "Now, answer my other questions. Was there anything I could have done differently that night or after you disappeared? And what do you need from me if this happens again?"

My fingers dig into her thigh. "No, sunshine. You did everything right that night and when I went radio silent. It was perfect. You didn't give up on me when I disappeared. You kept reaching out. I don't think there's anything you could have done. It's all on me. When you walked into the kitchen and slapped me, I should have pulled you into my arms and told you I love you and begged you to forgive me. Then I should have kissed you. Instead, I let you run out the door."

Her hands cradle my cheeks. "You love me?"

"Oh, sunshine. I thought love-at-first-sight was some insta-love book and movie bullshit until that first day on the street. I fell in love with a beautiful, free spirit, who dances on the street, changes popular song lyrics into a request for cake, and completely captivates my attention. I loved you before I knew your name."

"But you let me walk away that day, the night of the bachelorette party, and after our dive trip. That doesn't seem like love."

"You know why for the last one. The first two were because I knew I was in a shit situation, trying to figure out what I'm going to do with my life, and you're too young. I'm still wrestling with the age difference part of this. I'm thirty-eight. Thirty-nine in a few weeks. You're barely twenty-three. You should be with someone—"

Her hand covers my mouth, stopping my words. "Shut up. I refuse to hear anything about our age difference. Relationships should be built on common interests. We love all things outdoors, adventure, and travel. We are definitely sexually compatible. We have fun together. I know you get along with my brother. I'm sure I'll love your family." She removes her hand from my mouth. "Now, Griffin Henry Jameson, you only need to do one thing."

"What's that? I'll do anything you want."

"Take me home, get on your knees, and show me how much you deserve my forgiveness."

I rise to my feet, keeping her in my arms. "Do you have a bag or anything?"

"No. I only brought my phone."

I shift her to my back and piggyback carry her down the canyon path. When we get to the parking lot, I realize my Expedition is the only vehicle in the lot. "Where's your car?"

"At home. I walked."

I unlock the passenger door and set her on the seat. "Your place or mine, sunshine?"

"Yours is closer."

Chapter 19

When I told Griff he could get on his knees and show me how much he missed me and how sorry he was about pushing me away, I was joking. Sort of. Okay, not completely. But I didn't expect him to drop to his knees when we got into his room immediately. He wraps his arms around my waist and presses kisses against my stomach. "I'm so sorry, sunshine. I will never make you feel like you're not wanted again. Get naked. Let me show you how much I want you."

The only thing I want more than to strip naked and spend the night in his bed is to strip naked and take a shower. After days of little to no sleep and completely ignoring my self-care routine, I feel anything but sexy. I think I showered yesterday, but I can't be sure. I couldn't even drown my sorrows in my favorite dessert because I thought I might burst into tears if I saw one of the pink pastry boxes. Instead, I spent the last few days living off chips with salsa and queso. I ate ice cream by the pint right out of the container. Salsa and ice cream stains are splattered on the shirt that's technically his. I finally took that off after Devin left. I didn't take time to shower before heading to the restaurant because I was afraid I would chicken out and not confront Griff.

My hands press against his shoulders. "Stop, for just a few minutes. Let me steal a shower. I feel gross and not sexy. I need to feel sexy tonight."

He snakes up my body as he rises to his feet. "First, you are always sexy. Second, let me pamper you, sunshine. A long, hot bath, including a hair wash. A massage. The works."

I pull my shirt over my head and walk toward the ensuite bathroom. "You can spend the rest of the night on your knees next to the tub, washing my hair and then on the bed while you pamper me with a massage. That sounds like the best apology ever."

After a half-hour of soaking in the tub, I feel completely relaxed. Griff combs conditioner through my hair while we're standing at the sink. Then he braids my hair in the same double Dutch braids he did in the hotel room. When he's done, he kisses my shoulder. "Go crawl onto the bed. I'm going to get you water. You finished yours before we left the canyon."

When I get to the bedroom, I notice the door is open. Since I'm naked, I really don't want my brother to see me, so I walk over to close it and overhear Griff and

Devin. Maybe I shouldn't listen, but I know it's about me. Devin's voice is louder than Griff's. He sounds pissed. I know because he's doing that thing where he increases the volume of the words at the end of a sentence. It's something he learned from our dad. "When I told you to apologize, I didn't mean if you did, you'd have my blessing to fuck my sister. She deserves better. I know she thinks my rule about none of my employees dating her is misogynistic, but it's not why I do it. She deserves the fucking world. Not late nights, weird hours, a guy who barely sleeps. Someone who can give her everything, not someone who has to save each penny because the industry he loves is a shitstorm at best."

Griff keeps his voice calm. "First, I agree with you. I'm not good enough for her. But she thinks I am and is willing to deal with my grumpy disposition. In return, I'm going to talk to her about the things I push down and try to ignore. I already scheduled weekly sessions with my shrink again. Second, she does deserve everything, but Sadie doesn't want material things. She wants someone in her life who can't imagine her not being right next to him. She wants someone who loves the things she does and wants to spend every spare moment exploring with her. That's me. As for saving money, there was a time when I didn't have two nickels to rub together, but that's not me anymore. You don't have to worry about that. This is the only time I'm going to say anything about this, but what your sister and I do or don't do behind the bedroom door is only our business. Not yours. I don't plan to live in your spare room forever, but while I do, anything we choose to do will be out of your sight. You won't come home to find us on the couch or her laid out on the kitchen table or something."

That makes me laugh to the point I know they both hear me. I throw on one of Griff's shirts from the dresser and a pair of his boxers. Then I head down the hall. "Devin, he's right. I'm an adult. You're also right, I deserve the best. And he's it. He's a grumpy pain in my ass sometimes, but he's perfect for me."

As soon as I'm in reach, Griff wraps his arm around my waist. "Hey, sunshine. How much did you hear?"

My arms encircle his waist and I lean against his side. "All of it."

He places the water glass in my hands. "Drink this."

My brother unfolds his arms and waves his finger between us. "If you break her heart, I'll rip you apart."

"And I'll deserve it."

I finish chugging the water. "You'll have to beat me to him because if he pulls this shit again, I'm going full-on wrath of Sadie." I turn to face Griff. "If you think the slap in the kitchen hurt, you don't want to meet my uppercut or right hook."

Devin breaks into a smile for the first time since I told him a bit about what happened with Griff. "The girl can hit."

"Pretty sure she'll skin me alive if I even think about disappearing again." He pats my ass. "Bedtime, sunshine."

I step toward my brother. "Be nice. And stop treating me like I'm a child. You're going to have to learn to accept this."

He huffs, the way he does when he doesn't want to admit he's wrong. "I don't treat you like a child."

I quickly hug him. Before loosening my embrace, I whisper, "Yes, you do. Sometimes I love it, but not about this."

Then I walk down the hall to Griff's bedroom. This time I close the door so they can finish whatever needs to be said without me. When Griff crawls onto the bed next to me, he guides me into his arms. "I owe you a massage, but we're both exhausted. Let's save it for the morning."

"Sounds like a plan." Once I'm comfortable against him, he pulls the blanket over us. I press my lips to the center of his chest. "Goodnight."

"Night, sunshine."

I wake to an empty bed and the sounds of a ball bouncing against the floor. I expect to find Griff walking up and down the hall or pacing back and forth from one wall to the other in the living room. Instead, he's in the kitchen. He's sitting on the counter, with his earbuds in his ear, talking on the phone while bouncing the camo bouncing ball on the floor. When I realize he's on a call, I turn to leave the kitchen, but he stops me.

He reaches his arm out to me. "Good morning, sunshine."

I take his hand and let him guide me closer to him. "Morning."

He unmutes the call to say, "Sadie's awake. Can we continue this conversation later? I'm definitely interested. I can send you over the information you want and then we can set up a video chat or something with the team." Since he's using earbuds, I don't hear the other person. Griff smiles and nods at whatever is said. "Sounds like it could be a perfect fit. I really appreciate the opportunity. And I agree, either way, we need to plan something. Thanks again, Stefan. I look forward to talking to you again."

When he ends the call, he takes his earbuds out, hops off the counter, then lifts me into his arms. "If I didn't already love you, I would now that I know even when you were mad at me, you were helping me."

My legs wrap around his waist. "All I did was send Stefan what I knew about your background and ask him if he knew of anything that could work. I remember Paige mentioning Stefan was combat wounded too. He's happy with the company he works for. It was worth a shot."

He presses me against the wall and kisses me. When we part, I tighten my arms around his shoulders and rest my head against that perfect spot where his shoulder and neck meet. "Tell me about the job."

"The company sounds great. They're looking for someone with my secured communications experience. The best part is, it's not for a boots-on-the-ground type position. They are slowly transitioning the company to provide training. They have contracts with military, federal agencies, and law enforcement agencies." His entire face lights up as he tells me the details. "They're looking to expand their West Coast training team. Stefan's heading up the web security team. Based on my experience, he's recommending me for the communications position. Their communications expert lives in Georgia and wants to cover the South and East Coast. I'd be based wherever I want. I'd travel as needed."

"That sounds perfect. You could head back home and be near your family."

"I'm already home. Right here, with you in my arms. We'll make our home wherever you want to be."

Years ago, I wanted out of Ridgefield as soon as possible, but in the last three or four years, I've found my place here. I love my job and how each day is different. My coworkers are incredible. I can't imagine not living near Devin. "I want to stay here."

"Then we stay here. I love this town. I always have. I don't think we're ready to live together, but when we are, we'll find our own place." His hand wanders up my side. He cups my breast and gently squeezes. "I need to take you behind closed doors or we're going to risk breaking the promise to your brother."

"I don't think the promise said anything about not kissing me in the kitchen. It was specifically not spreading me out on the kitchen table. That sounds fun, by the way. We need to try that once one of us lives alone."

Griff shifts me so I'm over his shoulder and heads toward the bedroom. "Your brother leaves for a food and beverage convention on Wednesday. He'll be gone until Sunday. You're staying here while he's gone."

I smack his ass. "Yes, chef."

"Hopefully not chef for too much longer." He kicks the bedroom shut, then tosses me onto the bed. "I believe I owe you a massage."

I yank my shirt over my head before scampering across the room to the closet. "Later. Get naked. I want something else first."

"What are you doing?" he asks as he yanks his pants off and throws them into the hamper.

"Once you're naked, get on the bed."

I pull two of his ties from the hanger before turning toward him. I toss him the gray tie. "Tie me to the headboard with this one." Then the black one flies across the room. "I'm certain my brother doesn't want to hear me screaming. Put this one to good use, keeping my mouth shut."

Once I'm tied to the bed, he kisses me. "Any other requests?"

"Not this time. You already know what I like. Someday I want you to fill me with your cum, then watch it drip out of me. But we're not there yet."

"Someday, I'm taking you bare, but not yet. We haven't had the future talk yet, but we will. I need time to work through some things and adjust to my new life. Then, we can talk about what we want in terms of marriage, pets, and family. All I know for sure is you're mine for as long as you want to be."

"You're stuck with me forever. I don't know if I want a marriage and kids. It's not anything I've thought about much. Right now, the only thing I need is you. Let's live life together and let everything else fall into place."

His hand glides up my thigh. "Sounds perfect."

A half-hour later, my ankles are on his shoulders, the black tie balled in my mouth contains my moans, and his fingers dig into my hips while he plows into me. I haven't orgasmed yet, but I've been close countless times. Each time I think he's going to let it happen, he withdraws. Orgasm denial is cruel. But I know once I get to, it's going to rock through my body. I've read about tears during sex, but I've never experienced them until now.

He wipes them from my cheek, then pulls the tie from my mouth. "Soon, I'll let you come soon." His lips cover mine and he swallows the moans of ecstasy as he pushes into me again. This time he rubs my clit and I shatter.

When we both finish, he unties my wrists and lifts me into his arms, cradling me against his chest. "You are incredible." He wipes the sweat from my forehead and then kisses me. "Let's get cleaned up. Then I'll see what we have in the fridge and make us a late breakfast."

He lifts me into his arms and carries me into the shower. We quickly wash each other while kissing. I swear I'll never tire of having his lips on mine.

When we're both dressed, we head to the kitchen where we find my brother sitting at the table working on a puzzle book. He loves those murder mystery puzzles workbooks and keeps his nose shoved in one the way mine is always in a romance book. "I just pulled spinach frittata out of the oven. There's bacon. Sorry, Sadie. I'm out of the veggie stuff you like."

I grab three plates and serve frittata for all of us. I add bacon to two plates. "It's fine. This is plenty. I only eat one actual meal a day."

Griff's arms encircle my waist. "Not anymore. Proper meals, snacks when you're hungry, and plenty of water."

His lips press against my ear so my brother can't hear. "I plan on exhausting you regularly. You're going to need the energy. Take care of yourself."

He pours each of us coffee, then tops off Devin's mug while I bring plates to the table. The table only has two chairs, so I walk toward the couch, but Griff's arm hooks around my waist. His other hand taps his thigh. "Your seat's right here, sunshine."

Devin makes a fake gagging noise before taking a bite of his breakfast. "Oh, gross. You call her sunshine? Please don't tell me she calls you grumpy or grumpy bear or some other grumpy-sunshine romance trope bullshit."

I crack up and almost choke on my coffee. "I didn't even realize. I'm officially living my ideal book romance—grumpy-sunshine, brother's best friend, and age gap." I snap a piece of Griff's bacon into three pieces and chuck one at Devin. "And you said you didn't have a tattoo-covered friend to introduce me to."

"Well, I guess if my sister is going to get a real-life fairytale, it should be this one and not some Stockholm Syndrome dark romance or organized crime story where you end up chained in a basement."

Griff kisses my cheek. "Or tied to a bed while gagged." He winks as he squeezes my knee while I try to contain my laughter.

Chapter
20

When I asked Griff what he wanted to do for his birthday, his only response was, "You." I checked with his siblings and found out he's never been big on birthday celebrations. Growing up, they didn't host parties or make a big deal about the celebrations. Their mom made them their favorite cake. They got their favorite dinner, plus a few gifts. Birthdays were a big deal in our house. My dad went all out. We always had a party with friends the weekend before or after, plus dinner out on our birthday.

I want to do something special for Griff, but I also know he's not big on crowded places. Since his birthday is on a Monday, Forkn Spoon is closed. I invited everyone to join us on a trail ride through the canyon. My brother, Brit, Luke, Travis, and Kimber all agreed to join us. We did the five-mile ride and then headed to the picnic area where Kass and Hunter were waiting for us with lunch and dessert.

We end up one seat short around the table, so Griff pulls me onto his lap. "This is your seat. Thank you for planning this. Time with friends, hitting the trail, and delicious food is the perfect celebration. I couldn't ask for anything more."

I nuzzle my face against his neck, "Not even me wearing nothing but a ribbon tied in a bow?"

I feel his immediate reaction to that visual. He growls against my ear. "As soon as we get home, I want that."

My roommates are all working today, so we have the house to ourselves. "That's already the plan when we get to my place."

Splitting time between our two places is getting old, even though it's only been a few weeks. Thankfully, my roommates don't mind Jameson staying at the house. Dad offered me my childhood home whenever I wanted it. His tenants rent individual rooms and either rent for an entire school year or by the university quarter. That's an option whenever I'm ready. As much as I'd love to share a home with Griff, we aren't ready. We spend all of our spare time together and rarely spend a night apart, but we're still too new to cohabitate.

Once we're at the house, I run down the hall to my room and slam the door. "Don't come in here until I call you."

My impatient boyfriend taps his fingers against the door and huffs. "Fine. But I'm only counting to one-hundred. Then I'm opening this door."

I shimmy out of my clothes and run into the jack-and-jill bathroom between my room and Chelsea's. I'm gross after the ride. I know I don't have time for a shower, but I manage a washcloth bath in all the important areas.

"Fifty-two, fifty-three, fifty-four," Griff calls out through the door.

I slip into the red crotchless panties and garter belt set I bought at the boutique last week. Then I tie the extra wide ribbon around my boobs. Yesterday, I practiced a few times to be sure I could make it look like a fancy bow.

"Eighty-nine, ninety, ninety-one."

I pull the door open to discover I'm not the only one who changed. Griff is completely naked. His mouth hangs open as his eyes scan down my body. "Holy shit. You're always sexy, but damn. You about gave me a heartache dressing like that." He steps into the room and I close and lock the door. He takes my hand in his and turns me in a circle. "The most gorgeous present I've ever received."

"I'm glad you like it. I couldn't decide between the red and black."

"Red is definitely your color, sunshine. It looks fantastic against your sun-kissed skin." He sits on the edge of my bed and guides me onto his lap. "I'm going to spend the rest of my birthday kissing you."

"Hopefully not *just* kissing me. You can do whatever you want with me."

He drags the ribbon to untie the bow. "First, I'm going to spend a lot of time kissing, licking, and sucking these. Then I'm going to make you see stars." He sucks one nipple between his lips and gently bites while pinching the other.

My back arches and my head falls back. "That feels incredible."

His hand wanders down my torso until it reaches my aching pussy. He slowly tortures me with his fingers before finally giving me what I want. He quickly protects us with the condom I set on the bed before we left for the trail ride. He slides his cock inside me. "Ride me, sunshine."

Usually, he's the one in control. He gives me rough with restraints and leaves fingerprint-shaped bruises on my hips. But sometimes, when we're both craving intense connection, he gives me slower and makes it last even longer. Today, that's exactly what we desire. Just before we both finish, he tightens his arms around me and rotates us on the bed. I love feeling the weight of his body on top of me. He slides my calves up his sides until we're at the angle that always sends me over the edge. "Fuuuck," I cry out when the first wave of the orgasm hits.

By the time we finish, we're both breathless. He sucks my nipple into his mouth again before releasing it. "Best birthday celebration ever. I love you, sunshine."

"I love you too," I cup his cheeks in my hands and draw his face toward mine. "This is just the beginning of our celebrations together. Griffin Henry Jameson, I'm going to spend the rest of our lives celebrating how incredibly happy you make me."

He nuzzles his face against my chest. "Sounds like the perfect life, sunshine. I can't wait."

Epilogue

The last year was a whirlwind. I moved to Ridgefield thinking it was temporary while I figured out what I wanted to do now that the career I'd worked hard for wasn't an option. My temporary return to restaurant life lasted long enough for me to find the love of my life and find a new career with a security company. I'm now the West Coast Communications Training Director for a private security company. My team oversees training the agencies we contract with on all things related to secured communications.

I've spent the last three weeks on the road. The first week was our quarterly staff meeting at our corporate headquarters in New Orleans. Then I had a week in

Washington overseeing training with two agencies and then a few days in Utah before heading to Boise. The nice part about ending with Boise is Sadie's flying in and we're spending a long weekend with my family. My parents and siblings are excited to meet her face-to-face. We had planned to spend at least one holiday with them, but between storms closing roads and airports, and my work schedule, it didn't work out.

She's on the weekly family video call and is more active in the family group text chat than I am, so they all feel like they know her. When I said Sadie and I were staying at the hotel my company set me up in for the training, my mom and dad offered my childhood bedroom, which is now their guestroom. That room is across the hall from my parents. After three weeks apart, there is no way I can wait longer to have sex and I cannot have sex in my parents' house.

My sister-in-law sent Sadie a message and invited us to stay in the basement studio. They want as much time with us as possible this weekend. The studio is the better option, so I agreed to the request. I'm waiting at baggage claim and know when she's close because I feel it in my heart. As soon as I see her, she runs to me, shouting, "I missed you!"

I catch her in my arms and lift her off her feet. "I missed you too. Three weeks is too long. We can't be apart that long again." Once I set her down, I take her bag from her shoulder. "Did you check one too?"

She laces her fingers with mine. "No. It's only three nights. If I forgot something, I'll steal from you or go shopping."

"You already know you forgot something, don't you?"

"Toothbrush and pajamas."

I lead her to the rental car and help her into the front seat. "We'll swing by the store for a toothbrush and you don't need pajamas. You can sleep naked. I love you, sunshine."

"I love you too."

When we're done at the store, I drive out toward Garden City, where we're meeting my family. "Mom planned a family winetasting thing. We're doing a private tour and tasting at her favorite winery. She thought it would be a fun way to spend time together."

"I love that idea. I mentioned in the girl chat that I was nervous because I'm usually so shy in new situations."

"What girl chat?"

"Your sisters and sister-in-law added me to their girls-only chat. It's mostly how they plan surprises for your parents or bitch about your brother being a pain in the butt. Sounds like that gene runs strong with both the Jameson sons."

I squeeze her knee. "Behave."

"Make me," she smirks with a naughty eyebrow waggle.

After I park at the winery, I lean across the front seat and kiss her. "Let's go spend time with my family. We'll have time to drop off our stuff at my brother's before we go to dinner at Mom and Dad's."

I exit the car and walk around to her door. It took a few months of us being together for her to wait until I opened the door for her, but now it's a habit. I like taking care of her and little things like this are important to me. Before I take her hand in mine, I wipe the sweat from my hands on my jeans. I'm hoping she doesn't realize how nervous I am. Our families are already waiting for us on the outdoor patio, but she doesn't know that yet.

I lead her toward a narrow path that overlooks the vineyard. When she realizes we aren't walking toward the tasting room, she asks, "Where are we going?"

"We're a little early. I want to show you this. It's my favorite spot."

When we get to the end of the path, I position her so she's in front of me, and I drape my arm over her shoulder. "You shared your favorite view in Ridgefield with me. I want to share mine here with you."

She leans against me as I tighten my arm around her waist. "It's gorgeous. Makes me wish I brought my camera and not just my phone."

"Next time. I didn't even think of suggesting it."

I rest my chin on top of her head and take a deep breath. We haven't really talked about this since we decided we were just going to live life together and see how things went. I'm nervous that I'm moving too fast. She's still so young, but I'm ready. "Hey, sunshine. What are you doing next week?"

"Nothing special."

"And the week after that?"

"Just my regular schedule. Why?"

"What about three years from now? Any plans?"

She turns her head slightly to look at me over her shoulder. "What's going on?"

"Just wondering if you have plans for the rest of your life. If not, what do you think about spending all our days together?" I unclench my fist to reveal the ring. "Will you marry me?"

"Yes! I knew you would ask someday, but I wasn't expecting it this weekend."

I slide the ring onto her finger, and she gasps as she studies it. "I've never seen a ring like this."

"I couldn't find exactly what I wanted, so I had it made. The center stone is an oval-cut blue sandstone. It's dark and sparkly, like the night sky. The larger of the side stones are pear-cut alexandrite. The smaller stones are marquise-cut natural moss agate. My goal was for it to look like the galaxy in the center, with the colors of the ocean on each side."

"Mission accomplished on that. It represents everything I love. It's perfect." She drapes her arms over my shoulders, places her hands on the back of my neck, and guides my face toward hers. "I love you. I can't wait to be your wife."

My lips crash over hers. I spend the next ten minutes kissing my fiancée. Then I take her to celebrate with our families. The engagement isn't my only surprise. Her dad and brother flew in this morning so they could be here for the celebration. She'll see the last of the surprises later today when we're in the basement studio. Before I left Ridgefield, I spent a few hours on Poppy's table at Skin Deep. She filled in the remaining space on my back with a beautiful piece—the view from Sadie's favorite spot in the canyon with the sun shining above. I officially have my sunshine with me wherever I go.

The Ridgefield series is a Contemporary Romance, small-town series featuring connected standalone stories. There are three books planned for the main series, plus a spin-off series in the future.

Falling Into You is available here: *https://books2read.com/FallingIntoYou*

Falling Into You

Don't kiss your best friend's daughter is an unspoken rule of life. No one says the words aloud because everyone knows kissing someone young enough to be your child is wrong. After crossing the line, I knew the best thing to do was avoid her because one taste wasn't enough. But fate had other plans for us.

Jonah's a 48-year-old widower who lost his wife four years ago. He's filled his days with work, concerts, and solo travel. He figures he had his chance at a once-in-a-lifetime love.

Abigail's his best friend's 24-year-old daughter, who recently moved back to the area for a job she couldn't refuse.

She's a flannel-wearing, sweater-loving, pumpkin-everything fan who lives for caramel apples, bonfires, and candy corn.

The only thing he likes about the summer ending is ski season is only a few months away.

Their first encounter is at a banquet honoring her father. The next is at a dive bar concert for a band no one else wanted to see with them. A third chance meeting has them comparing schedules and deciding to attend events together instead of solo.

The last thing either of them expects is to fall harder than they think they should.

Running Into You

Jameson's life takes an unexpected turn when a career-ending injury forces him to reassess his future. Accepting his best friend's offer, he returns to the town he called home during college. His initial thought is that Ridgefield is a temporary layover while finding his footing, but fate has a different agenda and throws a captivating woman into his path multiple times.

Some call it fate.

Others call it serendipity.

Whatever it is, he knows it's trouble with a capital T.

Yet he can't deny the attraction, even when he discovers she's the one woman in Ridgefield he shouldn't pursue.

Running Into You is available here: *https://books2read.com/RunningIntoYou*

Leaning Into You

Olivia left her hometown in Kansas when she was eighteen. She's spent the last twelve years working hard to support her family from afar while striving for her goals in life. *Risqué Reads* is more than the bookstore she's dreamed of owning since high school. It's proof her ex-husband was wrong when he said she'd never make it without him.

When Olivia's life comes crashing down, the one person she's always been able to depend on is her older brother Jacob. But when tragedy strikes their family, she has to learn to live without him. She takes his request to heart and agrees to spend the next year focusing on living life in her family's new normal. The most unexpected part of the journey is discovering someone else has always cared about her. Her brother's best friend Mac.

He quickly becomes the one person she can lean on while she tries to hold her family together from afar.

Leaning   Into   You   is   available   here: www.books2read.com/LeaningIntoYou

You can find links to additional stories that take place in Ridgefield once available with the rest of JLynn's books here: https://linktr.ee/authorjlynnautumn

Acknowledgments

To my beta team and critique group, you are more than my readers, you are my friends. I couldn't continue to write without your support. Paige, your comments and assistance on plot and character development were beyond what I could have expected. 'Thank you' will never be enough. To my incredible editor, thank you for squeezing in this project and for editing it a second time when I decided to expand it into a *Ridgefield* series book. Lauren, you brought my vision for the cover and chapter headings to life. Thank you for your help.

Rumors is available now exclusively to newsletter subscribers.

Current subscribers claim your copy here: https://dl.bookfunnel.com/3n1bpunimx

New subscribers can sign up here and receive their copy: https://dl.bookfunnel.com/ubtzgrg0gb

Rumors is a standalone best friends to lovers, single dad romance novella with a guaranteed HEA. It features a heroine with a traumatic past and a protective hero who will do anything to make her feel safe again.

Tyler

We've been the talk of the town since we were teenagers. No one believes we are only friends. Everyone assumes we have some sort of friends with benefits relationship, but I don't care. Neither does she. I'd love to be more than best friends, but she lives by some ridiculous girl code. Since I dated her best friend in high school, we can never be more than friends. It's the dumbest rule I've ever heard. They're not even friends anymore. Because of those ten weeks, I'm stuck in friend zone hell for life.

Gwen

I've been in the friend zone for a decade. I shouldn't react like this anymore, but lately, his touches linger longer, he stands closer, and my body reacts quicker. I shouldn't like his hands on me. I have always been the friend. I'm the one he calls when he needs a babysitter. I'm the one who is fun to hang out with when he's not looking to get laid. I've never been the girl he looks at as anything more than a best friend. I'm the girl who will forever be in the friend zone. Years ago, I had to decide if that was enough. My head knows I made the right choice. My guards are up to protect my heart. If only my body would cooperate and stop sparking from every simple touch.

When Tyler makes it clear how he feels about Gwen, she worries she can't give him every part of a relationship because of her past trauma. He's willing to try at her pace, if she'll give him the chance he's waited a decade for.

ALSO BY JLynn

JLynn Autumn is a part-time author who dreams of the day she can be a full-time author. She's a lifelong bookworm, a reader, a writer, and an advocate. She's passionate about social justice, education reform, and special education service equity. She is married to her "game changer," the man who showed her that being made a priority and being treated with respect should be the standard, not the exception. They have one daughter, who is sassy, bossy, and opinionated, and keeps them on their toes. JLynn believes that coffee and tea are magical liquids that bring her to life most mornings; pizza and tacos should be their own food groups; late nights are always better than early mornings; houseplants are a waste of space that will always be forgotten about; and poodles and poodle mixes are the best pets. She's a huge fan of snark, sarcasm, and happily ever after in real life and books.

Her favorite tropes to write are friends to lovers, single parents, workplace romance, and small town. She loves writing heroines with haunting pasts who find their strength by finding their voice, and heroes who love the women in their lives with every part of them and take care of the people in their lives. Her stories are filled with friendship and love, and show that real-world problems have a place in fiction. The goal of each story she writes is to prove happily ever after exists.

Sign-Up for JLynn's Newsletter to stay up to date on release, pre-orders, and promotions: http://eepurl.com/hlS5IL

Jabbering with JLynn Facebook Group: https://www.facebook.com/groups/jabberingwithjlynn

Facebook Author Page: https://www.facebook.com/authorjlynnautumn
Instagram: https;//www.instagram.com/authorjlynnautumn
Bookbub: https://www.bookbub.com/profile/jlynn-autumn

Also By JLynn Autumn

Links to all of JLynn's stories can be found here:
https://linktr.ee/authorjlynnautum

Woods Lake Series

Welcome to Woods Lake, a small town outside a big city, where lifelong friendships are formed and happily ever after still exists. The Woods Lake series is a series of connected standalone novels with recurring characters. Each book tells the story of one couple, including their happily ever after.

Jenna's Monsters

Jenna's Monsters is the prequel to the *Woods Lake Series* books. It tells Marco & Jenna's history told through a collection of Marco's memories. Marco was sixteen when he met Jenna. At the time, she was his best friend's little sister. Over the years, their relationship changed. They saw each other through their best and worst moments. No longer just his friend's sister, she's his best friend, and the person he promised he'd always protect.

It's Always Been You

Marco has loved Jenna since he was 16 and she was 12. When Ricky died, his mom had Jenna move into their house because she had nowhere else safe. Marco held her every night when the nightmares came for the next year. The friendship has always felt like it was destined to be more, but the timing was never right. Can their 14-year friendship survive the relationship trial he requests? Will this week-long trial be what they need to make things work finally, or will they lose each other in the process?

You Mean Something

Can a guy who's never committed to anything more than a fun weekend or two weekends, at most, become boyfriend material? Jesse's never wanted to try, but for Lexie, he's willing to and hopes that she considers him more than just a distraction from the drama in her life.

A Woods Lake Christmas

A Woods Lake Christmas is a standalone Christmas novella that features all of the main characters in the Woods Lake series as they each decorate for Christmas and then come together as a family on Christmas Eve and Christmas Day.

I Never Stopped Loving You

An epic love story of two people who love each other in a way that most people only dream of, but years of distance becomes unbearable and leads them to drift apart. Is their love strong enough to overcome this time apart and find their second chance at a happily ever after?

Like Nothing Before

Micah and Shauna are the outgoing, adventurous couple both inside and outside the bedroom and sparks fly immediately in this couple's story. Shauna always told herself and everyone else that she was the girl who wanted to work and travel. She didn't want a piece of paper and a commitment. She didn't want kids. When she realizes that she was wrong and she does want all of those things, she wonders if Micah wants all of that too. Micah's the greatest guy she's ever known and the first person to see her as more than a fun fling, so can't imagine her life without him, but also can't imagine not having the happily ever after that she never knew she wanted. Can a girl who's never committed to anything more than a fun weekend or a week, find the happily ever after she was certain she never wanted?

Everything I've Waited For

Matt had wished on stars every night since his mom walked out when he was a kid. He used his childhood wishes to ask for his mom to come back. Teenage Matt wished for a baseball career. Professional baseball player Matt has spent the past decade wishing for someone to love for the rest of his life. As soon as Matt meets Mel, he knows his star wish came true. Mel is a self-described daytime dreamer and nighttime wisher. After leaving an abusive relationship and overcoming a slip into past bad habits, she's spent her nights wishing for a family. Her daydreams are filled with images of a houseful of babies, a yard filled with toys, and most of all, someone to love who will love her completely and make her feel safe. She can't understand why Matt wants her when he can have anyone, but she's so thankful he did.

Back to You

Lucy's life is a rollercoaster—the highs are epic; the journey to the top is exciting; the drop varies from a little scary to downright terrifying; and the bottom is a soul-crushing disappointment. Her rollercoaster life is easier with someone who will hold her through the scary parts.

Tony's the only person who has ever loved all of her scary parts. Life is easier with Tony and he'd never do anything to hurt her, but her mind messes with her and makes her doubt everything about herself, him, and their relationship. For over four years, he woke up every day and fought for them. No matter how many times she slipped and fell into old habits, he fought. Nine months ago, Lucy walked out and that time, Tony didn't chase her—he let her leave. Now, it's Lucy's turn to fight for them. She's determined to do it and hopefully, it's not too late.

Unexpected Love

I forced my best friend's little sister to move in with me when she became a single mom. I wasn't supposed to fall in love with her.

A Woods Lake Wedding

Leave it to the two people who didn't believe in happily ever after, marriage vows, or wedding bands to plan a destination wedding. Will's determined to give Kayla the wedding of her dreams and keep his promise to her brothers that they can be there. Just a few weeks after he proposed, he's planned a wedding that will exceed Kayla's dreams.

Game Changer Series

Game Changer

After breaking up with her boyfriend of six years, Kris accepts a transfer to her company's San Francisco office, fulfilling her childhood dream of living in her favorite city.

Jonathan works 80-100 hours a week most weeks, and no woman he's ever met has understood or accepted that. He likes the idea of a long-term relationship but never seemed to have time for anything more than a few weeks before work got in the way.

Kris and Jonathan are assigned to team up on a year-long project. Their non-work talk lunch rule develops into a friendship that feels like more. Can Kris trust him enough to tell him why she doesn't go to her hometown and the secret she's been keeping from almost everyone who knew
her before moving to San Francisco?

Forever Series
The *Forever Series* is a small-town, second-chance novella series that each answer a different question as the couple's navigate their second chance.

Resisting Forever answers the question 'What happens when your idea of happily ever after isn't a ring and marriage vows?' It's available wide now. www.books2read.com/ResistingForever
    Chasing Forever answers the question 'What if you weren't ready for forever and she was?' www.books2read.com/ForeverSeries2

    Finding Forever answers the question 'What if the only thing standing between you and forever is your age difference?' www.books2read.com/ForeverSeries3

Choosing Forever is the paperback collection of the *Forever Series* and includes the bonus story *Rediscovering Forever* which answers the question 'What if you made a choice when you were a teenager and chose the wrong forever?' www.books2read.com/ForeverSeries4

Gracie's

Gracie's is a series of connected standalone novellas features staff and customers at Gracie's bar.

Breaking the Rules

When Cami was 19, she almost asked her brother's best friend to teach her everything he knew about the bedroom. 5 years later when she finds out he doesn't have bedroom experience, she offers to be his bedroom tutor on a one-week wedding party trip.

The rules are simple: 7 days, 7 lessons, no falling in love.

Weekend Wedding Vows

I'm not the girl guys date. I'm not the girlfriend. I'm the friend with benefits. Or the friend who was briefly something more. I'm the girl who is pretty enough to sleep with on a weeknight, but not take out on weekends. I'm the girl who they'll cuddle with on the couch while watching a movie, but who they don't take out to dinner. I'm the one they call last minute when plans fall through, but who isn't pretty enough to make plans with in advance. I'm the placeholder between relationships. Maybe it's my turn to use a placeholder.

Christmas in Camden

Becca works long hours at a job she's good at but hates. She longs for a slower pace of life for her daughter. When her aunt and uncle ask her to come to their ranch for the holidays, she thinks it's because it's been too long since they visited. She doesn't know they have a plan and job offer that would bring her back permanently. Then Clint drops a bombshell when he tells Becca the only regret he has in life is not coming to get her when she became a single mom.

Twelve years ago, Clint watched Becca walk away from

him. He refused to be the reason she didn't pursue her dreams. Now she's home for the holidays, and he's not letting her leave without telling her everything he wanted to that day. He's determined to give every reason to stay this time.

Tropes: Small-Town Romance; Second-Chance Romance; Friends-to-Lovers Romance; Closed Door Romance; Single-Parent Romance; Sweet Romance.